MISS READ'S
CHRISTMAS TALES

MISS READ'S
CHRISTMAS TALES

Village Christmas · The Christmas Mouse

Miss Read

Illustrations by John S. Goodall

HOUGHTON MIFFLIN COMPANY

Boston   New York   1995

For information about permission to reproduce selections from this book, write to Permissions, Houghton Mifflin Company, 215 Park Avenue South, New York, New York 10003.

For information about this and other Houghton Mifflin trade and reference books and other multimedia products, visit The Bookstore at Houghton Mifflin on the World Wide Web at http://www.hmco.com/trade/.

The moral right of the author has been asserted.

Library of Congress Cataloging-in-Publication Data
Read, Miss.
Miss Read's Christmas tales / illustrations by John S. Goodall.
p.   cm.
Contents: Village Christmas — The Christmas mouse.
ISBN 0-395-75289-2 (cloth). — ISBN 0-395-74131-9 (pbk.)
1. Christmas stories, English. 2. Country life — England —
Fiction. 3. Mice — Fiction.
PR6069.A42A6 1995
823'.914 — dc20   95-34784
CIP

Printed in the United States of America
QUM 10 9 8 7 6 5 4 3 2 1

CONTENTS

VILLAGE
CHRISTMAS

To Jill and John
with love

THE DARKNESS THROBBED with the clamour of church bells. The six sonorous voices of St Patrick's peal chased each other, now in regular rhythm, now in staccato clashes, as the bell-ringers sweated at their Christmas peal practice.

The night was iron-cold. Frost glittered on the hedges and fields of Fairacre although it was not yet eight o'clock. Thatched roofs were furred with white rime beneath a sky brilliant with stars. Smoke rose in unwavering blue wisps from cottage chimneys, for the air was uncannily still.

The sound of the bells carried far in such weather. At Beech Green, three miles away, Miss Clare heard them clearly as she stooped to put her empty milk bottle tidily on her cottage doorstep, and she smiled at the cheerful sound. She knew at least four of those six bell-ringers for she had taught them their lessons long ago at Fairacre school. Arthur Coggs, furtively setting rabbit snares by a copse near Springbourne, heard them as clearly. The shepherd, high on the downs above the village, and the lonely signalman tending his oil-lamps on the branch line which meandered along the Cax valley to the market town, heard them too.

Nearer at hand, in the village of Fairacre, the bells caused more positive reactions. The rooks, roosting in the topmost boughs of the elm trees hard by the reverberating belfry, squawked an occasional protest at this disturbance. A fox, slinking towards Mr Willet's hen run, thought better of it as the bells rang out, and beat a retreat to the woods. Mrs Pringle, the dour cleaner of Fairacre school, picked up a flake of whitewash with disgust from the spotless floor where it had fluttered from the quaking kitchen wall, and a new baby nearby, awakened by the clamour, wailed its alarm.

Miss Margaret Waters and her sister Mary were quietly at work in their cottage in the village street. They sat, one each side of the big round table in the living room, penning their Christmas cards in meticulous copper plate. Music tinkled from the large old-fashioned wireless set on the dresser by the fireplace, vying with the noise of the bells outside. Mary's grey curls began to nod in time to a waltz, and putting her pen between her teeth, she rose to increase the volume of the music. At that moment an excruciating clashing of St Patrick's peal informed the world of Fairacre that at least three of the six bell-ringers were hopelessly awry in their order.

'Switch it off, Mary, do! Them dratted bells drowns anything else. We may as well save the electric!' exclaimed Margaret, looking over the top of her gold-rimmed spectacles.

Mary obeyed, as she always did, and returned to

her seat. It would have been very nice, she thought privately, to hear 'The Merry Widow' waltz all the way through, but it was not worth upsetting Margaret – especially with Christmas so near. After all, it was the season of goodwill. She picked up a card from the central pile and surveyed it with affection.

'All right for Uncle Toby?' she queried, her head on one side. 'He's partial to a robin.'

Her sister looked up from her writing and studied the card earnestly. Sending just the right card to the right person was something which both sisters considered with the utmost care. Their Christmas cards had been chosen from the most modestly priced counter at Bell's, the Caxley stationer's, but even so the amount had been a considerable sum from the weekly pension of the two elderly sisters.

'You don't feel it's a mite spangly? That glitter on the icicles don't look exactly *manly* to me. I'd say the coach and horses myself.'

Mary set aside the robin reluctantly, and began to inscribe the card with the coach and horses:

From your affectionate nieces,
Margaret and Mary

The ancient mahogany clock, set four-square in the middle of the mantelpiece, ticked steadily as it had done throughout their parents' married life and their own single one. A log hissed on the small open fire, and the black kettle on the trivet began to hum. By bedtime it would be boiling, ready for the sisters' hot water bottles. It was very peaceful and warm in the cottage and Mary sighed with content as she tucked in the flap of Uncle Toby's envelope. It was the time of day she loved best, when the work was done, the curtains were drawn, and she and Margaret sat snugly and companionably by the fire.

'That seems to be the lot,' she observed, putting the envelopes into a neat stack. Margaret added her last one. Three, including the rejected robin, remained unused.

'There's bound to be someone we've forgot,' said Margaret. 'Put 'em all on the dresser, dear, and we'll post 'em off tomorrow.'

The church bells stopped abruptly and the room seemed very quiet. Ponderously and melodiously the old clock chimed half past eight from the mantelpiece, and Mary began to yawn. At that moment there came a sharp rapping at the door. Mary's mouth closed with a snap.

'Who on earth can that be, at this time of night?' she whispered. Her blue eyes were round with alarm. Margaret, made of sterner stuff, strode to the door and flung it open. There, blinking in the sudden light, stood a little girl.

'Come in, do, out of the cold,' begged Mary, who had followed her sister. 'Why, Vanessa, you haven't got a coat on! You must be starved with the cold! Come by the fire now!'

The child advanced towards the blaze, plump hands outstretched like pink star-fish. She sniffed cheerfully and beamed up at the two sisters who looked down at her with so much concern. The child's two front milk teeth had recently vanished and the gap gave her wide smile a gamin air. She shook the silky fringe from her sparkling eyes. Clearly, Miss Vanessa Emery was very happy to be inside Flint Cottage.

'And what do you want, my dear, so late in the day?' enquired Margaret, unusually gentle.

'Mummy sent me,' explained the child. 'She said could you lend her some string to tie up Grandpa's parcel. *Thick* string, she said, if you could manage it. It's a box of apples, you see, off our tree, and sticky tape won't be strong enough on its own.'

'Indeed it won't,' agreed Mary opening the dresser drawer and taking out a square tin. She opened it and placed it on the table for the child to inspect. Inside were neat coils of string, the thickest at the left-hand side and the finest – some of it as thin as thread – in a tidy row on the right-hand. The child drew in her breath with delight and put a finger among the coils.

'Where did you buy it?' she asked.

'*Buy* it?' echoed Margaret, flabbergasted. 'Buy *string?* We've never bought a bit of string in all our borns! This comes off all the parcels that have come here over the years.'

'Mum cuts ours off and throws it away,' explained

the child unabashed. She picked up a fat gingery coil of hairy twine and examined it closely.

'Could you spare this?' she asked politely.

'Of course, of course,' said Mary, hurrying to make amends for the horrified outburst from her sister. She tucked it into the pocket on the front of the child's cotton apron.

'And now I'll see you across the road,' she added, opening the front door. 'It's so late I expect you should be in bed.'

The child left the fire reluctantly. One hand gripped the string inside her pocket. The other she held out to Margaret.

'Good night, Miss Waters,' she said carefully, 'and thank you for the string.'

'You're welcome,' replied Margaret, shaking the cold hand. 'Mind the road now.'

The two sisters watched the child run across to the cottage opposite. It sat well back from the village street in a little hollow surrounded by an overgrown garden. Against the night sky its thatched roof and two chimneys gave it the air of a great cat crouched comfortably on its haunches. They heard the gate bang, and turned again to their fire, slamming the door against the bitter cold.

'Well!' exploded Margaret. 'Fancy sending a child out at this time of night! And for a bit of string! "Cuts it off" indeed! Did you ever hear of such a wicked waste, Mary?'

'Dreadful!' agreed her sister, but with less vehemence. 'And that poor little mite with no coat on!'

'Well, I've always said, there's some people as have no business to be parents and them Emerys belong to 'em. Three under seven and another on the way! It's far too many. I feel downright sorry for that poor unborn. She can't look after the three she's got already!'

Margaret picked up the poker and rapped smartly at a large lump of coal. It split obediently and burst into joyous flame. The kettle purred with increased vigour, and Margaret moved it further back on the trivet.

The two sisters sat down, one at each side of the blaze. From the cupboard under the dresser Mary drew forth a large bundle, unrolled it and gave one end to Margaret. They were making a hearthrug, a gigantic monster of Turkish design, in crimson and deep blue. Each evening the sisters spent some time thrusting their shining hooks in and out of the canvas as they laboriously added strand after strand of bright wool.

Margaret's end was growing much more quickly than Mary's. Her hook moved more briskly, with sharp staccato jabs, and the wool was tugged fiercely into place. Mary moved more slowly, and she fingered each knotted strand as though she loved it. She would be sorry when the work was finished. Margaret would be glad.

'I must say, they seem happy enough,' observed Mary, reverting to the topic of the Emerys. 'And very healthy too. They're dear little girls – and so polite. Did you notice the way Vanessa shook hands?'

'It's not the children I'm criticizing,' replied Margaret. 'It's their parents. There'll be four little mites under that roof soon, and dear knows how many more to come. And they don't seem to have any idea of bringing them up right! Look at their fancy names, for one thing! Vanessa, Francesca, Anna-Louise – I ask you!'

'I rather like them,' said Mary with spirit. Margaret snorted and jabbed the canvas energetically.

'And all dressed up in that frilly little apron with a heart-shaped pocket, and no decent warm coat on the child's back,' continued Margaret, now in full spate. 'It's all on a par with the house. All fancy lampshades, and knick-knacks hanging on the wall, and great holes in the sheets, for all to see, when she hangs 'em on the line. 'Twasn't no surprise to me to hear she cuts up her string and throws it out. We done right, Mary, not to get too familiar with her. She's the sort as would be in here, everlasting borrowing, given half a chance, as I told you at the outset.'

'I dare say you're right, dear,' responded Mary equably. She usually was, thought Mary, pensively. They worked in silence and Mary looked back to the time when the Emerys had first arrived in Fairacre, three months before, and she had watched from a vantage point behind the bedroom curtain their furniture being carried up the brick path.

It was a golden afternoon in late September and

Margaret had gone to St Patrick's to help with the decorations for Harvest Festival. A bilious headache had kept Mary from accompanying her, and she had retired to bed with an aspirin and a cup of tea.

She had slept for an hour and the sound of children's voices woke her. At first she thought the school-children must be running home, but it was only three o'clock by the flowered china timepiece on the mantelshelf, and she had gone to the window to investigate.

A dark green pantechnicon almost blocked the village street. The men were staggering to the house opposite with a large and shabby sideboard between them. Two little girls danced excitedly beside them, piping shrilly to each other like demented moorhens. Their mother, cigarette in mouth, watched the proceedings from the side of the doorway.

Mary was a little shocked – not by the cigarette, although she felt that smoking was not only a wicked waste of money but also very unhealthy – but at the young woman's attire. She wore black tights, with a good-sized hole in the left leg, and a short scarlet jerkin which ended at mid-thigh. Her black hair was long and straight, and her eyes were heavily made up. To Mary she appeared like an actress about to take part in a play set in the Middle Ages. No one – absolutely no-one – dressed like that in Fairacre, and Mary only hoped that the young woman would not hear the remarks which must inevitably come from such village stalwarts as Mrs Pringle and her own sister, if she continued to dress in this manner.

Nevertheless, Mary was glad to see that they had neighbours, and gladder still to see that there were children. The thatched cottage had stood empty all the summer, ever since the old couple who had lived there from the time of their marriage in good Queen Victoria's reign, had departed to a daughter's house in Caxley and had moved from thence to Fairacre churchyard. It would be good to see a light winking through the darkness again from the cottage window, and to see the neglected garden put into order once more, thought Mary.

Her headache had gone and she straightened the bed coverlet and made her way down the steep dark staircase. She was pleasantly excited by the activity outside the front door, and tried to hear what the children were saying, but in vain. A thin wailing could be heard and, peeping out from behind the curtain, Mary saw that the woman now had a baby slung over her shoulder and was patting its back vigorously.

'Three!' breathed Mary, with delight. She was devoted to children and thoroughly enjoyed taking her Sunday School class. To be sure, she was often put out when some of the bigger boys were impudent, and was quite incapable of disciplining them, but small children, and particularly little girls of gentle upbringing, delighted her warm old spinster's heart.

When Margaret returned she told her the good news. Her sister received it with some reserve.

'I'll be as pleased as you are,' she assured Mary, 'if they behaves themselves. But let's pray they ain't the squalling sort. You can hear too much in that bedroom of ours when the wind's that way.'

'I wondered,' began Mary timidly, 'if it would be a kindness to ask 'em over for a cup of tea when we makes it.'

'If she was alone,' replied Margaret after a

moment's consideration, 'I'd say "Yes," but with three children and the removal men too, I reckons we'd be overdone. Best leave it, Mary – but it does you credit to have thought of it.'

Mary was about to answer, but Margaret went on. Her expression was cautious.

'We don't want to be too welcoming yet awhile, my dear. Let's see how they turn out. Being neighbourly's one thing, but living in each other's pockets is another. Let 'em get settled and then we'll call. Best not to go too fast or we'll find ourselves baby-sitting every evening.'

A thought struck her.

'Seen the man, Mary?'

Mary admitted she had not.

'Funny!' ruminated her sister. 'You'd have thought he'd be on hand.'

'Maybe he's clearing things up the other end,' suggested Mary.

'Maybe,' agreed Margaret. 'I only hope and pray she's not a widow woman, or worse still one that's *been left*.'

'We'll soon know,' replied Mary comfortably, well versed in village ways. Fairacre had a lively grapevine, and there would be no secrets unhidden in the cottage opposite, the sisters felt quite sure.

Within a week it was common knowledge that the Emerys had moved from a north London suburb – Enfield, according to Mrs Pringle, Southgate, by Mr Willet's reckoning, though the Vicar was positive that it was Barnet. Much to Margaret's relief, Mr Emery had appeared, and her first glimpse of him was as he put out the milk bottles the next morning whilst still clad in dashing crimson pyjamas with yellow frogging.

He worked 'up the Atomic', as did many other Fairacre residents, but drove there in a shabby old Daimler about nine, instead of going on the bus which collected the other workers at seven-thirty each morning.

'One of the high-ups,' commented Mr Willet. 'Had a bit of book-learning in science and that, I don't doubt. Looks scruffy enough to have a degree, to my mind. Wants a new razor-blade, by the looks of things, and that duffle coat has seen a few meals down it.'

Fairacre was inclined to agree with Mr Willet's somewhat tart summing-up of Mr Emery, though the female residents pointed out that he seemed to take his share of looking after the children and, say what you like, he had very attractive thick black hair. It was Mrs Emery who provided more fodder for gossip.

As Mary had foreseen, her Bohemian garments scandalized the older generation. And then, she was so breath-takingly friendly! She had introduced herself to Mr Lamb in the Post Office, and to two venerable residents who were collecting their pensions, shaking hands with them warmly and asking such personal questions as where they lived and what were their names.

'Wonder she didn't ask us how old we be,' said one to the other when they escaped into the open air. 'She be a baggage, I'll lay. I'll take good care to steer clear of that 'un.'

She hailed everyone she met with equal heartiness, and struck horror into every conservative Fairacre

heart by announcing her decision to join every possible club and society in the village 'to get to know
people', and her intention of taking the little girls with
her if the times of the meetings proved suitable.

'Terribly important for them to make friends,'
she told customers and assistants in the village shop
one morning. Her wide warm smile embraced them
all. She seemed unaware of a certain frostiness in
the air as she made her purchases, and bade them all
good-bye, with considerable gusto, when she left.

Margaret and Mary viewed their ebullient neighbour with some alarm. Three days after her arrival,
when Margaret was already planning the best time
to call, Mrs Emery knocked briefly on the sisters'
front door and almost immediately opened it herself.

'Anyone at home?' she chirped blithely. 'Can I
come in?'

Before the startled sisters could reply, she was in
the room, with two beaming little girls following
her.

'I'm your new neighbour, as I expect you know,'
she said, smiling disarmingly. 'Diana Emery. This is
Vanessa, and this one Francesca. Say "Hello", dar-
lings.'

'Hello!' 'Hello!' piped the two children.

Mary collected her wits with remarkable com-
posure. She found the Emery family attractive, despite their forward ways.

'There now!' she began kindly. 'We were wondering when to call and see you. Won't you take a cup
of coffee? Margaret and I usually have some about
this time.'

'I'll get it,' said Margaret swiftly, glad to escape
for a moment to take stock of the situation. Mary

could see from her expression that she was not pleased by the invasion.

'Lovely!' sighed Mrs Emery, flinging off a loose jacket of jade green, and settling in Margaret's armchair. The two little girls collapsed cross-legged on the hearth-rug and gazed about them with squirrel-bright eyes beneath their silky fringes.

'What about the baby?' asked Mary, concerned lest it should have been left outside. The morning was chilly.

'Not due until the New Year,' replied Mrs Emery nonchalantly. 'And jolly glad I shall be when it's arrived.'

There was a gasp from the doorway as Margaret bore in the tray. She was pink, and obviously put out. Mary hastened to explain.

'I meant the *third* little girl,' she said.

'Oh, Anna-Louise! She's fast asleep in the pram. Quite safe, I can assure you.'

'We want a brother next time,' announced Vanessa, eyeing the plate of biscuits.

'Three girlth ith three too many,' announced Francesca. 'Thatth's what my daddy thayth.'

'That's a joke, explained Vanessa.

'Sometimes I wonder,' their mother said, but her tone was cheerful.

Margaret poured coffee and tried to avert her eyes from Mrs Emery's striped frock which gaped widely at the waist fastening, displaying an extraordinary undergarment of scarlet silk. Could it *possibly* be a petticoat, Margaret wondered? Were there really petticoats in existence of such a remarkable colour?

Mary did her best to make small talk. It was quite apparent that Margaret was suffering from shock, and was of little help.

'Is there anything you want to know about the village? Perhaps you go to church sometimes? The services are ten-thirty and six-thirty.'

'We're not much good at church-going,' admitted their neighbour. 'Though I must say the Vicar looks a perfect poppet.'

Margaret swallowed a mouthful of coffee too quickly and coughed noisily. This was downright sacrilege.

'Gone down the wrong way,' explained Francesca, coming close to her and gazing up anxiously into Margaret's scarlet face. Speechless, but touched by the child's solicitude, Margaret nodded.

'And if you want to go to Caxley,' continued Mary, 'there is a bus timetable on the wall of "The Beetle and Wedge". Is there anything else we can help you with?'

Mrs Emery put her cup carelessly upon its saucer so that the spoon crashed to the floor. Both children pounced upon it and returned it to the table.

'Well, yes, there is something,' said their mother. 'Could you possibly change a cheque for me? I'm absolutely out of money and want to get some cigarettes. Edgar won't be home until eight or after.'

There was a chilly silence. The sisters had no banking account, and the idea of lending money, even to their nearest and dearest, was against their principles. To be asked, by a stranger, to advance money was profoundly shocking. Margaret found her tongue suddenly.

'I'm afraid we can't oblige. We keep very little in the house. I suggest that you ask Mr Lamb. He may be able to help.' Her tone was glacial, but Mrs Emery appeared unperturbed.

'Ah well,' she said cheerfully, struggling from the armchair and gaping even more hugely at the waist band, 'never mind! I'll try Mr Lamb, as you suggest. Must have a cigarette now and again with this brood to look after.'

She picked up the green jacket and smiled warmly upon the sisters.

'Thank you so much for the delicious coffee. Do pop over and see us whenever you like. We'll probably be seeing quite a bit of each other as we're such close neighbours.'

And with these ominous words she made her departure.

Ever since then, thought Mary, busily prodding her hook in the rug, she and Margaret had fought a polite, but quietly desperate, battle against invasion.

'Be friendly to all, but familiar with few,' said an old Victorian sampler hanging on their cottage wall.

The sisters found its advice timely. The children, they agreed, were adorable, and although they appeared far too often for 'a-shilling-for-the-electricity-meter' or 'a-box-of-matches-because-the-shop's-shut' and other like errands, the two sisters had not the heart to be annoyed with them. In any case, it was simple to dismiss them when their business was done, with a piece of chocolate to sweeten their departure.

Mrs Emery, growing weekly more bulky, was more difficult to manage, and the two sisters grew adept at making excuses. Once inside, she was apt to stay over an hour, seriously throwing out the working of the sisters' day. She certainly was an embarrassment as a neighbour.

Mary's eyes strayed to the table, and the rejected Christmas card with the gay robin among his spangles. A thought struck her, and she put down her hook.

'Margaret,' she said suddenly, 'what about sending that robin to the Emery children?'

Margaret began to look doubtful.

'Well, my dear, you know what a mite of trouble we've had with that woman! I just wonder –'

'Oh, do now!' pressed Mary, her face flushed. ''Tis Christmas! No time for hard thoughts, sister, and them children would just love it. I could slip over with it after dark on Christmas Eve and pop it through the letter box.'

Margaret's face relaxed into a smile.

'We'll do it, Mary, that we will!'

She began to roll up the rug briskly, as the church clock struck ten. Mary gave a happy sigh, and lifted the singing kettle from the trivet.

'Time for bed,' she said, taking two hot water bottles from the bottom of the dresser cupboard. 'Think of it, Margaret! Only three more days until Christmas!'

The next three days were busy ones for the ladies at Flint Cottage. Red-berried holly, pale mistletoe and glossy ivy were collected, and used to decorate the living room. Two red candles stood one at each end of the mantelpiece, and a holly garland hung from the brass knocker on the front door.

The cake was iced, the pudding fetched down from the top shelf in the pantry, the mincemeat jar stood ready for the pies and a trifle was made. One of Mrs Pringle's chickens arrived ready for the table, and sausage meat came from the butcher.

Margaret crept away privately while Mary was bringing in logs from the woodshed, and wrapped up two pairs of sensible lisle stockings which she had bought in Caxley for her sister's present. Mary took advantage of Margaret's absence at the Post Office and swiftly wrapped up a pair of stout leather gloves and hid them in the second drawer of the bedroom chest.

All Fairacre was abustle. Margaret and Mary helped to set up the Christmas crib in the chancel of St Patrick's church. The figures of Joseph, Mary and the Child, the shepherds and the wise men reappeared every year, standing in the straw provided by Mr Roberts the farmer, and lit with sombre beauty by discreetly placed electric lights. The children came in on their way from school to see this perennial scene, and never tired of looking.

The sisters helped to decorate the church too. There were Christmas roses on the altar, their pearly beauty set off by sprigs of dark yew amidst the gleaming silver ware.

On Christmas Eve the carol singers set out on their annual pilgrimage round the village. Mr Annett, the choir master, was in charge of the church choir and any other willing chorister who volunteered to join the party. This year, the newcomer Mr Emery was among them, for word had soon got round that he sang well and Mr Annett had invited him to join the carol singers. Clad in the duffle coat which Mr Willett thought of so poorly, he strode cheerfully along the frosty lanes of Fairacre, swinging a hurricane lamp as though he had lived in the village all his life, and rattling away to his companions with the same friendly foreign loquacity as his wife's.

One of their stopping places was outside. 'The Beetle and Wedge', strategically placed in the village street. Margaret and Mary opened their window and watched the singers at their work. Their breath rose in silver clouds in the light of the lanterns. The white music sheets fluttered in the icy wind which spoke of future snow to the weather-wise of Fairacre. Some of the lamps were hung on tall stout ash-sticks, and these swayed above the ruffled hair of the men and the hooded heads of the women.

Mr Annett conducted vigorously and the singing was controlled as well as robust. As the country voices carolled the eternal story of joyous birth, Mary felt that she had never been so happy. Across the road she could see the upstairs light in the bedroom of the Emery children, and against the glowing pane were silhouetted two dark heads.

How excited they must be, thought Mary! The stockings would be hanging limply over the bed rail, just as her own and Margaret's used to hang so many years ago. There was nothing to touch the exquisite anticipation of Christmas Eve.

'Hark the herald angels sing,
Glory to the new-born King,'

fluted the choir boys, their eyes on Mr Annett, their mouths like dark Os in the lamplight. And the sound of their singing rose like incense to the thousands of stars above.

On Christmas morning Margaret and Mary were up early and went to eight o'clock service. A feeling of night still hung about the quiet village, although the sun was staining the eastern sky and giving promise of a fine day ahead.

The lighted crib glowed in the shadowy chancel like the star of Bethlehem itself, and the aromatic smell of the evergreens added to the spirit of Christmas. Later, the bells would ring out and the winter sunshine would touch the flowers and silver on the altar with brightness. All would be glory and rejoicing, but there was something particularly lovely and holy about these quiet early morning devotions, and the two sisters preferred to attend then, knowing that the rest of the morning would be taken up with the cheerful ritual of Christmas Day cooking.

They unwrapped their few parcels after breakfast, exclaiming with genuine pleasure at the modest calendars and handkerchiefs, the unaccustomed luxury of richly perfumed soap or chocolates which friends and relatives had sent.

Margaret thanked Mary warmly for the gloves. Mary was equally delighted with her stockings. They exchanged rare kisses and told each other how lucky they were.

'There's not many,' said Margaret, 'as can say they live as contented as we do here. And under our own roof, thank God, and nothing owing to any man!'

'We've a lot to be thankful for,' agreed Mary, folding up the bright wrappings neatly. 'Best of all each other – and next best, our health and strength, sister.'

'Now, I'm off to stuff the bird,' announced Margaret, rising with energy. 'I'll put on the pudding too while I'm in the kitchen. Must have that properly hotted up by midday.'

She bustled off and Mary began to make up the fire and sweep the hearth. The two red candles looked brave and gay, standing like sentinels each side of the Christmas cards ranged along the mantelpiece. She wondered if the Emery children had liked the fat robin. She could see them now, in imagination, surrounded by new Christmas presents, flushed and excited at the joy of receiving and of giving.

At that moment, a rapping came at the front door and she rose from her sweeping to open it. Vanessa stood there, looking far from flushed and excited. The child's eyes were large with alarm, her face pale with cold and fright.

'What is it, my love? Come in quickly,' cried Mary.

'It's Mummy. She said, "Could you come over, please?" She's ill.'

'Is Daddy with her?' asked Margaret, appearing in the doorway with her fingers pink and sticky with sausage meat.

'No. He's had to go to Grandma's. Grandpa rang up last night after we'd gone to bed. Grandma's being stroked.'

'Had a stroke,' corrected Margaret automatically. 'Dear me, that's bad news! We'll be over as soon as we've put the dinner in.'

The child's eyes grew more enormous than ever. She looked imploringly at Mary.

'But it's the baby coming! You must come this minute. Please, *please!*'

Without a word Margaret began to take off her kitchen apron.

'Go over, Mary,' she said quietly. 'I'll follow you.'

Indescribable chaos greeted Mary's eyes when she stepped into the Emery's kitchen. It was a large square room with a brick floor, and comfortably warmed by an Esse cooker appallingly streaked with grime. Quantities of anthracite dust were plentifully sprinkled on the floor at its base, and had been liberally trodden about the room.

The débris of breakfast littered the table, and coloured paper, tags and string garnished sticky cereal bowls and mugs. A ginger cat lapped up some milk which dripped from an overturned jug, and the confusion was made more acute by Francesca who stood proudly holding a new scarlet scooter, ringing the shiny bell without cessation.

'Give over, do!' begged Mary, peremptory in her flurry. The child obeyed, still beaming. Nothing could quench her Christmas bliss, and Mary was immediately glad to see that this was so. The sound of Anna-Louise's wailing became apparent, and Mary opened the door of the box staircase and began to mount. The two little girls started to follow her.

'You stop here, there's dears,' said Mary, much agitated. Who knows what terrors might be aloft? 'Pick up the paper and make it nice and tidy.'

To her relief they fell upon the muddle joyously, and she creaked her way above. Mrs Emery's voice greeted her. She sounded as boisterous as ever, and Mary's fears grew less. At least she was conscious!

'You are a darling! You really are!' cried Mrs Emery. She was standing by the window, a vast figure in a red satin dressing gown embroidered on the back with a fierce dragon. Mary suddenly realized how very young she looked, and her heart went out to her.

'We were so sorry to hear about your mother-in-law,' began Mary, a little primly.

'Poor sweet,' said Mrs Emery. 'It *would* have to happen now. Edgar went off as soon as he came back from carol-singing. And then, this! *Much* too early. I suppose I've got the dates wrong again. Ah well!'

She sighed, and suddenly clutched the front of her dressing gown again. Mary felt panic rising.

'Do get into bed, there's a love,' she begged, turning back the rumpled bedclothes invitingly. The bottom sheet had a tear in it six inches long, and a very dirty rag doll with the stuffing coming out. Mary was appalled. She must put something clean on the bed! Suppose the baby was born in that unhygienic spot! She looked for help towards Mrs Emery, who was bowed before the chest of drawers and gasping in an alarming way.

'You must have clean sheets,' announced Mary with an authoritative ring in her voice which wholly surprised her.

'Cupboard,' gasped Mrs Emery, nodding towards the next room.

An unpleasant smell was the first thing that Mary noticed about the adjoining bedroom. Anna-Louise was standing in a cot. Her nightgown and the bedding were ominously stained, but her cries had ceased and she threw Mary a ravishing smile.

'You pretty thing,' cried Mary, quite entranced. 'Aunt Mary'll see to you in just a minute.'

She swiftly ransacked the cupboard. She found a roll of mackintosh sheeting and two clean linen ones. Bustling back to the bedroom she set about making the bed with vigorous speed. Mrs Emery was upright again, leaning her damp forehead against the cool window-pane. She consented to be led to the bed, unprotesting, and let Mary remove the flamboyant dressing gown.

'There, there!' soothed Mary, tucking her in as though she were a child. 'I'll bring you a drink.'

'I'm all right now,' whispered the girl, and at that moment Margaret appeared.

'Does nurse know?' was her first remark. Mary felt suddenly guilty. Of course it was the first thing she should have found out. Trust Margaret to know exactly what to do!

'Yes,' replied Mrs Emery. 'At least, someone at her house does. Nurse was out on another baby case. They were sending word.'

'What about Doctor Martin?' continued Margaret.

'Nurse will get him, if need be,' said the girl. She sank back on the pillow and suddenly looked deathly tired. 'It won't come for hours,' she told them. 'It's just that I was worried about the children.'

'I know, I know,' said Margaret gently. 'We'll look after them all right. Leave it all to us.'

'Anna-Louise needs a wash,' said Mary, retiring to the next room. She beckoned Margaret to follow her, and closed the door between the two rooms.

'What on earth shall we do?' she implored Margaret. Margaret, for once, looked flummoxed.

'Dear knows, and that's the honest truth,' admitted her sister. 'Let's hope nature knows best and nurse comes pretty smartly. This is foreign stuff to us, Mary, but we must hold the fort till help comes.'

She turned to survey Anna-Louise who was jumping rhythmically up and down in the cot, with dire results.

'Land's sake, Mary!' That child wants dumping in the bath – and the bedding too!'

'I'll do her,' said Mary swiftly. 'And then I can keep an eye on Mrs Emery up here. You see to things downstairs.'

'Won't do no harm to give nurse another ring,' observed Margaret, turning to the door. She looked back at her sister.

'Who'd a thought we'd a been spending Christmas like this?'

She vanished downstairs and Mary went to turn on the bath for her charge.

Anna-Louise, well-soaped, was absolutely adorable. Fat and pink, with a skin like satin, she made Mary a willing slave. She patted the water vigorously, sending up showers of spray, and drenching Mary kneeling beside the bath. Mary could have stayed there all day, murmuring endearments and righting the celluloid duck time and time again. But the water cooled rapidly, and there was much to do. She gathered the naked child into a grubby bath towel, and dried her on her lap.

'She hasn't had her breakfast yet,' Mrs Emery said drowsily when the child was dressed. She looked at her daughter with amusement.

'That's Francesca's jumper,' she observed, 'but no

matter. Tie a bib on the poor lamb. She's a filthy feeder.'

Below stairs, all was amazingly quiet. The table had been cleared and the two little girls were blissfully engaged in filling in their new Christmas drawing books with glossy long crayons as yet unbroken. Margaret was busy sweeping the floor with a broom from which most of the bristles had long vanished.

'Has the baby come yet?' asked Vanessa, without looking up from the mad oscillation of her crayoning.

'Not yet,' replied Mary, threading Anna-Louise's fat legs through her high-chair. She stood back and surveyed the baby anxiously. 'And what does Anna-Louise like for breakfast?'

Francesca put down her crayon and gazed earnestly at her younger sister.

'She liketh bacon rindth betht,' she told Mary.

'Well, we've no time to cook bacon,' said Margaret flatly, still wielding the broom.

'Egg,' said Vanessa briefly. 'All horrible and runny. That's what she likes.'

The sisters exchanged questioning glances.

'Sounds reasonable,' muttered Margaret, 'if you can find the egg saucepan.'

'It's the milk one as well,' volunteered Vanessa, making for a cupboard. 'Here you are.' She produced a battered saucepan with a wobbly handle, and returned to the drawing book.

'Did you get through to nurse?' asked Mary agitatedly, as she filled the saucepan.

'Still out. Message supposed to have been passed on. I reckons we ought to get her husband back. It's his business after all.' Margaret spoke with some asperity.

'I'll go and ask Mrs Emery,' said Mary, 'while the egg boils.'

She returned to the bedroom to find Mrs Emery humped under the bedclothes with her head in the pillow. She was groaning with such awful intensity that Mary's first impulse was to fly for Margaret, but she controlled it. She patted the humped back consolingly and waited for the spasm to pass. Somewhere, far away it seemed, the bells of St Patrick's began to peal for morning service. A vivid picture of the peaceful nave, the holly and the Christmas roses, the fragrance of the cypress and yew, came clearly to Mary, standing helplessly there watching her neighbour in labour. How long ago, it seemed, since she and Margaret knelt in the church! Yet only three or four hours had gone by.

The spasm passed and Diana Emery's face appeared again.

'Better,' she said. 'Can I have that drink now? Coffee, please – no milk. Any sign of that confounded nurse?'

'She's on her way,' said Mary. 'And we thought we ought to phone your husband.'

'His parents aren't on the telephone,' said Mrs Emery.

'We could ring the police,' suggested Mary with sudden inspiration. Mrs Emery laughed with such unaffected gaiety that Mary could hardly believe that she had so recently been in such pain.

'It's not *that* serious. Nurse will be along any minute now, and think how wonderful it will be to present Edgar with a fine new baby!'

She sounded so matter-of-fact and cheerful, that Mary gazed at her open-mouthed. Was child-bearing really undertaken so lightly? She remembered Margaret's tart comments on people who had large families with such apparent fecklessness. How many more would there be in this casual household, Mary wondered? Then she remembered the sight of Anna-Louise in the bath and hoped suddenly, and irrationally, that there would be more – lots more – and that she would be able to enjoy them.

'I'll get your coffee, my love,' she said warmly and went below.

Returning with the steaming black brew, she remembered something.

'Shouldn't we put the baby's things ready for nurse?' she asked.

'There's not a great deal,' confessed the girl, warming her hands round the cup. 'I intended to do most of the shopping after Christmas in Caxley. So many people about, I just couldn't face it.'

'But you must have *some* things,' persisted Mary aghast.

'In the bottom drawer,' said the girl vaguely. 'And

there are lots of Anna-Louise's things that will do, in the airing cupboard.'

Mary was shocked at such a slapdash approach to an important event, and her face must have shown it, for Mrs Emery laughed.

'After the first you don't bother quite so much,' she confessed. 'You can get by with all the odds and ends the others had.'

Mary found six new nappies in the drawer, and a bundle of small vests, some tiny night-gowns yellow with much washing, and a shawl or two, in the airing cupboard.

'And what shall we put the baby in?' she inquired.

'Anna-Louise's carry-cot. It's in her room. It probably wants clean things in it.' The girl had slipped down into the bed again and closed her eyes. She looked desperately tired, thought Mary, with a pang.

The carry-cot held two dolls, a headless teddy-bear and a shoe, all carefully tucked up in checked tablecloth. Mary took it downstairs to wash it out and dry it ready for the new occupant.

'If that dratted nurse don't come soon,' said Margaret, 'I'll fetch Doctor Martin myself, that I will! I'll just slip over home, Mary, and turn that bird and add a mite of hot water to the pudding.'

'We'll never have a chance to eat dinner, sister,' cried Mary. 'Not as things are!'

'There's them three to think of,' replied Margaret nodding to the children. 'We've got them to feed, don't forget.'

She lifted the latch and hurried across to their cottage. One or two parishioners, in their Sunday best, were making their way to church. Mary saw Mr and Mrs Willet stop to speak to her sister as she stood with one hand on the door knob. There was much headshaking, and Mrs Willet looked across at the Emery's house with some alarm.

'The news will soon be round Fairacre,' thought Mary, as she dried the carry-cot.

It was clean and peaceful now in the kitchen, and she noticed the paper chains festooned against the ceiling, and the Christmas cards pinned along the rafters. Her own fat robin was there, and she glowed with pleasure. Vanessa and Francesca were still engrossed in their artistic efforts, and Anna-Louise wiped her eggy plate with her fingers and sucked them happily. What dear good children they were, thought Mary!

At that moment she heard their mother calling from overhead. Her voice sounded shrill and desperate. Mary took the stairs at a run. The girl was sitting up in bed, clenching and unclenching her hands on the coverlet.

'You *must* get that nurse – or the doctor, or someone. I can't stick this now. It's coming pretty fast.'

'I'll ring again,' promised Mary, thoroughly frightened by the urgency of the girl's pleas. 'Just lie down again. I'm sure it's better. Can I do anything? Rub your back, say, or bring you a hot bottle?'

She did her best to appear calm, but inwardly terror gripped her. Supposing the baby came this minute? What on earth did you do with a new-born baby? Wasn't there something about cutting a cord? And if so, where did you cut it? And how did you tie it up afterwards? Hadn't she heard once that mothers bled to death if the cord wasn't tied properly? And that wretched carry-cot wouldn't be anywhere near aired, let along made up with clean bedding, if the baby arrived now! Mary found herself shaking with panic, and praying desperately. Don't let it come yet, please, dear Lord! Not until nurse arrives, please God!

'There, my love —' she began, when she stopped abruptly. The door of the staircase had opened and someone was mounting.

'Margaret!' she cried. 'Quickly, Margaret!'

A sturdy figure appeared in the doorway.

'Nurse! Thank God!' cried Mary, and began to weep.

'You go and make us all a cup of tea,' said Nurse Thomas with gruff kindness. And Mary fled.

An hour later, Margaret and Mary sat at their own table, serving three excited little girls with Christmas dinner. Nurse's car still stood outside the cottage opposite, but Doctor Martin's was not to be seen. Evidently all was going well, and nurse had everything well in hand.

Mary found herself as excited as the children. What a relief it was to be home again, and to know that Mrs Emery was being properly nursed! It was impossible to eat amidst such momentous happenings, and she was glad to neglect her own plate and to have the pleasant task of guiding Anna-Louise's teaspoon in the right direction.

In the afternoon the youngest child slept soundly in Mary's own bed. St Patrick's clock chimed three, and still no message came from the house across the road.

A few Fairacre folk began to go by, taking an afternoon stroll for the sake of their digestions, between Christmas dinner and the further challenge of iced cake for tea. They noted nurse's car and the light in the upstairs window, and fell to wondering.

Margaret was reading 'The Tale of Two Bad Mice' from a new glossy copy which the children had received that morning, when a tapping came at the door. Mrs Lamb from the Post Office stood outside with a posy of anemones in her hand. She caught sight of the two little girls inside and spoke in a whisper.

'For their mother, my dear. Hope all's going well. We heard about it after church. You're going over again, I expect?'

'Yes indeed,' answered Margaret, accepting the bright bunch. 'She'll be pleased with these. Nurse is still there, as you see.'

She nodded towards the car.

'Give Mrs Emery our best wishes,' said Mrs Lamb. 'Poor soul, without her husband too! She's got everyone's sympathy, that's a fact.'

She set off homeward, and Margaret returned to

the fireside. It began to grow dark, for the afternoon
was overcast, and Mary took a taper and lit the
bright red candles. The flames stretched and
dwindled in the draught and the little girls gazed at
them starry-eyed.

'Do you always have candles?' asked Vanessa. 'Or
just at Christmas?'

'Just at Christmas,' said Margaret.

She put down the book and gazed at the bright
flames with the children. The waiting seemed end-
less, and suddenly she felt desperately tired. How
much longer, she wondered, before they knew?

Just then they heard the sound of a gate shutting
and footsteps coming to their door. The two sisters
exchanged swift glances. Could it be –?

Mary opened the door and there stood the nurse,
smiling.

'Come in,' said Mary.

'I daren't. I'm late now,' said nurse, 'but all's well.'

Margaret and the children gathered at the door.

'A boy,' nurse announced proudly. 'Seven pounds

and bonny. And Mrs Emery's asleep. Can one of you go over?'

'You go,' said Margaret to Mary. 'I'll bring the children over later.'

'We want to see him,' pleaded Vanessa.

'*Now!*' added Francesca stubbornly.

'Now!' echoed Anna-Louise, not understanding the situation, but glad to try a new word.

'Later on,' responded nurse firmly. 'Your mummy's tired.'

She turned to go and then looked back.

'Mr Emery rang up. I've told him the news and he'll be back very soon.'

She waved and made her way across the road to the car.

'Tell Mr Emery I'll be in, in the morning,' she called, and drove off in a cloud of smoke.

As if by magic, two heads popped out from the doorway of 'The Beetle and Wedge'. They belonged to the landlord and his wife.

'Couldn't help seeing nurse go off,' he said to Mary. 'What is it?'

'A boy!' said Mary, smiling.

'Now, ain't that good news?' beamed his wife. 'You tell her we'll be wetting the baby's head in here tonight.'

'Ah, she's a grand little mother, for all her funny ways,' declared her husband. 'Tell her it'll be nice to have another young 'un in the village.'

Mary tiptoed into the silent cottage. Everything seemed to slumber. The cat slept on a chair by the stove. Nothing moved.

She left the door of the staircase ajar so that she

could hear the slightest sound from above, and sat down at the table.

In the domestic stillness which enveloped her, after the stress of the day, old and lovely words came into her mind.

'And it came to pass, while they were there, the days were fulfilled that she should be delivered.

'And she brought forth her first-born son; and she wrapped him in swaddling clothes, and laid him in a manger, because there was no room for them in the inn.'

Mary sat motionless savouring the age-old miracle of the Nativity. And here, in this house, was another Christmas baby! She felt that she could not wait another moment. She must see him.

She slipped off her stout country shoes and tiptoed up the stairs. It was very quiet in the bedroom. Mrs Emery, looking pathetically young and pale, slept deeply. Beside the bed, on two chairs, was the carry-cot.

Mary leant over and gazed in wonder. Swaddled tightly, in the shawl she had found for him in the airing cupboard, was the new-born baby, as oblivious of the world about him as his sleeping mother.

Mary's heart beat with such fervour that she wondered that the sleepers did not wake. Full of joy, she crept below once more, and in her dizzy head beat the words:

'And the angel said unto them, Be not afraid; for behold, I bring you good tidings of great joy which shall be to all people.'

There was a sound outside, and she looked up from lacing her shoes. There stood Mr Emery, his face alight.

'Where is she?' he asked.

'They're both upstairs,' whispered Mary, and opened the staircase door so that he could go aloft and see his son.

Late that night, the two sisters sat each side of the hearth, working at their rug.

'D'you know what Vanessa said when her father fetched her?' asked Margaret. 'She said: "This is the loveliest Christmas we've ever had!" 'Twas good of the child to say it, I thought, after such a muddling old day. It touched me very much.'

'She spoke the truth,' replied Mary slowly. 'Not only for herself, but for all of us here in Fairacre. 'Tis a funny thing, sister, but when I crept up the stairs to take a first look at that new babe the thought came to me: "Ah! You're a true Fairacre child, just as I was once, born here, and most likely to be bred up here, the Lord willing!" And then another thought came: "You've warmed up us cold old Fairacre folk quicker'n the sun melts frost." You know,

Margaret, them Emerys have put us all to shame, many a time, with their friendly ways, and been snubbed too, often as not. It took a Christmas baby to kindle some proper Christmas goodwill in Fairacre.'

''Tis true,' admitted Margaret, putting down the rug hook, and gazing into the dying fire. Into her tired mind there floated irrelevant memories . . . Mrs Emery's scarlet petticoat, a ginger kitten lapping milk, Anna-Louise fumbling with her egg-spoon, while her sisters watched her with squirrel-bright eyes, laughing at her antics . . . all adding up to colour and warmth and gentle loving-kindness.

'Now this has happened,' she said soberly, 'It won't stop at *Christmas* goodwill, sister. The Emerys are part and parcel of this village for good. There's room for all sorts in Fairacre, Mary, but it took a newborn babe to show us.'

She began to roll up the rug briskly.

'Come, sister. Time we was abed.'

THE
CHRISTMAS MOUSE

To Elizabeth Ann Green
who started this story

CHAPTER 1

The rain began at noon.

At first it fell lightly, making little noise. Only the darkening of the thatched roofs, and the sheen on the damp flagstones made people aware of the rain. It was dismissed as 'only a mizzle'. Certainly it did not warrant bringing in the tea towels from the line. Midday meals were taken in the confident belief that the shower would soon blow over. Why, the weathermen had predicted a calm spell, hadn't they, only that morning?

But by two o'clock it was apparent that something was radically wrong with the weather forecast. The wind had swung round to the northwest, and the drizzle had turned to a downpour. It hissed among the dripping trees, pattered upon the cabbages in

cottage gardens and drummed the bare soil with
pock marks.

Mrs Berry, at her kitchen window, watched the
clouds of rain drifting across the fields, obscuring
the distant wood and veiling the whole countryside.
A vicious gust of wind flung a spatter of raindrops
against the pane with so much force that it might
have been a handful of gravel hurled in the old
lady's face. She did not flinch, but instead raised her
voice against the mounting fury of the storm.

'What a day,' said Mrs Berry, 'for Christmas
Eve!'

Behind her, kneeling on the rush matting, her
daughter Mary was busy buttoning her two little
girls into their mackintoshes.

'Hold still,' she said impatiently, 'hold still, do!
We'll never catch the bus at this rate.'

They were fidgeting with excitement. Their cheeks

were flushed, their eyes sparkling. It was as much as they could do to lift their chins for their mother to fasten the stiff top buttons of their new red mackintoshes. But the reminder that the bus might go without them checked their excitement. Only two afternoon buses a week ran past the cottage, one on market day, and one on Saturday. To miss it meant missing the last-minute shopping expedition for the really important Christmas presents – those for their mother and grandmother. The idea of being deprived of this joy brought the little girls to partial submission.

Mary, her fingers busy with the buttons, was thinking of more mundane shopping – Brussels sprouts, some salad, a little pot of cranberry jelly for the turkey, a few more oranges if they were not too expensive, a lemon or two. And a potted plant for Mum. A cyclamen perhaps? Or a heather, if the cyclamen proved to be beyond her purse. It was mean the way these florists put up the prices so cruelly at Christmas. But there, she told herself, scrambling to her feet, the poor souls had to live the same as she did, she supposed, and with everything costing so much they would have to look after themselves like anyone else.

'You wait here quietly with Gran for a minute,' she adjured the pair, 'while I run and get my coat on, and fetch the baskets. Got your money and your hankies? Don't want no sniffing on the bus now!'

She whisked upstairs and the children could hear her hurrying to and fro above the beamed ceiling of the kitchen.

Old Mrs Berry was opening her brown leather purse. There were not many coins in it, and no notes, but she took out two silver fivepenny pieces.

'To go towards your shopping,' said the old lady. 'Hold out your hands.'

Two small hands, encased in woollen gloves knitted by Mrs Berry herself, were eagerly outstretched.

'Jane first,' said Mrs Berry, putting the coin into the older girl's hand. 'And now Frances.'

'Thank you, Gran, thank you,' they chorused, throwing their arms round her comfortable bulk, pressing wet kisses upon her.

'No need to tell your mum,' said Mrs Berry. 'It's a little secret between us three. Here she comes.'

The three hurried to the cottage door. The rain was coming down in sheets, and Mary struggled with an umbrella on the threshold.

'Dratted thing' – she puffed – 'but can't do without it today. I'll wager I forget it in some shop, but there it is. Come on now, you girls. Keep close to me, and run for it!'

Mrs Berry watched them vanish into the swirling rain. Then she shut the door upon the weather, and returned to the peaceful kitchen.

She put her wrinkled hand upon the teapot. Good, it was still hot. She would have another cup before she washed up.

Sitting in the wooden armchair that had been her husband's, Mrs Berry surveyed the kitchen with pleasure. It had been decorated a few years before and young Bertie, Mary's husband, had made a good job of it. The walls were white, the curtains cherry-red cotton, and the tiles round the sink were blue and white. Bertie, who had set them so neatly, said they came from a fireplace over in Oxfordshire and were from Holland originally. The builder, a friend of his, was about to throw them out but Bertie had rescued them.

A clever boy with his hands, thought Mrs Berry, stirring her tea, though she could never understand what poor Mary saw in him, with that sandy hair and those white eyelashes. Still, it did no good to think ill of the dead, and he had made a good husband and father for the few short years he and Mary had been married. This would be the third Christmas without him – a sad time for Mary, poor soul.

Mrs Berry had once wondered if this youngest daughter of hers would ever marry. The two older girls were barely twenty when they wed. One was a farmer's wife near Taunton. The other had married an American, and Mrs Berry had only seen her twice since.

Mary, the prettiest of the three girls, had never been one for the boys. After she left school, she worked in the village post office at Springbourne, cycling to work in all weather and seeming content to read and knit or tend the garden when she returned at night.

Mrs Berry was glad of her daughter's company. She had been widowed in 1953, after over thirty years of tranquil marriage to dear Stanley. He had been a stonemason, attached to an old-established firm in Caxley, and he too cycled daily to work, his tools strapped securely on the carrier with his midday sandwiches. On a day as wild and wet as this Christmas Eve, he had arrived home soaked through. That night he tossed in a fever, muttering in delirium, and within a week he was dead – the victim of a particularly virulent form of influenza.

In the weeks of shock and mourning that followed, Mary was a tower of strength to her mother. Once the funeral was over, and replies had been sent to all the friends and relatives who had written in sympathy, the two women took stock of their situation. Thank God, the cottage was her own, Mrs Berry said. It had taken the savings of a lifetime to buy when it came on the market, but now they had a roof over their heads and no weekly rent to find. There was a tiny pension from Stanley's firm, a few pounds in the post office savings bank, and Mary's weekly wage. Two mornings of housework every week at the Manor Farm brought in a few more shillings for Mrs Berry. And the farmer's wife, knowing her circumstances, offered her more work, which she gladly accepted. It was a happy household, and Mrs Berry was as grateful for the cheerful company she found there as for the extra money.

Mother and daughter fell into a comfortable routine during the next few years. They breakfasted together before the younger woman set off on her bicycle, and Mrs Berry tidied up before going off to her morning's work at the farmhouse. In the afternoon, she did her own housework, washed and ironed, gardened, or knitted and sewed. She frugally made jams and jellies, chutneys and pickles for the store cupboard, and it was generally acknowledged by her neighbours that Mrs Berry could stretch a shilling twice as far as most. The house was bright and attractive, and the door stood open for visitors. No one left Mrs Berry without feeling all the better for her company. Her good sense, her kindness and her courage brought many people to her door.

Mary had been almost thirty when she met Bertie

Fuller. He was the nephew of the old lady who kept the Springbourne post office and had come to lodge with her when he took a job at the Caxley printing works.

Even those romantically inclined had to admit that nothing as fantastic as love at first sight engulfed Mary and Bertie. She had never been one to show her feelings and now, at her age, was unlikely to be swept off her feet. Bertie was five years her senior and had been married before. There were no children of this first marriage, and his wife had married again.

The two were attracted to each other and were engaged within three months of their first meeting.

'Well, my dear, you're old enough to know your own mind,' said Mrs Berry, 'and he seems a decent, kindly sort of man, with a steady job. If you'd like to have two rooms here while you look for a house you're both welcome.'

No, the villagers agreed, as they gossiped among themselves, Mary Berry hadn't exactly caught 'a regular heart-throb', but what could you expect at thirty? She was lucky really to have found anyone, and they did say this Bertie fellow was safe at the printing works, and no doubt was of an age to have sown all the wild oats he wanted.

The wedding was as modest as befitted the circumstances, and the pair were married at Caxley registry office, spent their brief honeymoon at Torquay, and returned to share the cottage with old Mrs Berry. It was October 1963 and the autumn was one of the most golden and serene that anyone could recall.

Their first child was due to arrive the following September. Mary gave up her job at the post office in June.

The summer was full of promise. The cottage garden flowered as never before, and Mary, resting in a deck chair, gazed dreamily at the madonna lilies and golden roses, and dwelt on the happy lot of the future baby. They had all set their hearts on a boy, and Mary was convinced that it would be a son. Blue predominated in the layette that she and Mrs Berry so lovingly prepared.

When her time came she was taken to the maternity wing of the local cottage hospital, and gave birth to a boy, fair and blue eyed like his father. She held him in her arms for a moment before returning him to the nurse's care. In her joy she did not notice the anxious looks the doctor and nurse exchanged. Nor did she realize that her child had been taken from her bed straight to an oxygen tent.

In the morning, they broke the news to her that the boy had died. Mary never forgot the utter desolation that gripped her for weeks after this terrible loss. Her husband and mother together nursed her back to health, but always, throughout her whole life, Mary remembered that longed-for boy with the blue gaze, and mourned in secret.

A daughter, Jane, was born in the spring of 1966, and another, Frances, in 1968. The two little girls were a lively pair, and when the younger one was beginning to toddle, Bertie and Mary set about finding a cottage of their own. Until that time, Mrs Berry had been glad to have them with her. Mary's illness, then her second pregnancy, made her husband and mother particularly anxious. Now, it seemed, the time had come for the young family to look for their own home. Mrs Berry's cottage was becoming overcrowded.

The search was difficult. They wanted to rent a house to begin with, but this proved to be almost impossible. The search was still on when the annual printing-house outing, called the wayzgoose, took place. Two buses set off for Weymouth carrying the workers and their wives. Mary decided not to go on the day's outing. Frances had a summer cold and was restless, and her mother had promised to go to a Women's Institute meeting in the afternoon. So Bertie went alone.

It was a cloudless July day, warm from the sun's rising until its setting. Mary, pushing the pram along a leafy lane, thought enviously of Bertie and his companions sitting on the beach or swimming in the freshness of the sea. She knew Weymouth from earlier outings and loved its great curved bay. Today it would be looking its finest.

The evening dragged after the children had gone to bed. Usually, the adults retired at ten, for all rose early. On this evening, however, Mrs Berry went upstairs alone, leaving Mary to await Bertie's coming. Eleven o'clock struck, then twelve. Yawning, bemused with the long day's heat, Mary began to lock up.

She was about to lock the front door when she heard a car draw up. Someone rapped upon the door, and when Mary opened it, to her surprise she saw Mr Partridge, the vicar, standing there. His kind old face was drawn with anxiety.

'I'm sorry to appear so late, my dear Mrs Fuller, but a telephone message has just come to the vicarage.'

'Yes?' questioned Mary. The vicar looked about him in agitation.

'Do you think we might sit down for a moment?'
Mary remembered her manners.

'Of course; I'm so sorry. Come in.'

She led the way into the sitting room, still bewildered.

'It's about Bertie,' began the vicar. 'There's been
an accident. I fear. Somewhere south of Caxley.
When things were sorted out, someone asked me to
let you know that Bertie wouldn't be home tonight.'

'What's happened? Is he badly hurt? Is he dead?
Where is he?'

Mary sprang to her feet, her eyes wild. The vicar
spoke soothingly.

'He's in Caxley hospital, and being cared for. I
know no more, my dear, but I thought you would
like to go there straight away and see him.'

Without a word Mary lifted an old coat from the

back of the kitchen door. The vicar eyed her anxiously.

'Would it not be best to tell Mrs Berry?' he suggested.

She shook her head.

'I'll leave a note.'

He waited while she scribbled briefly upon a piece of paper, and watched her put it in the middle of the kitchen table.

'No point in waking her,' she said, closing the front door softly behind her.

The two set off in silence, too worried to make conversation. The air was heavy with the scent of honeysuckle. Moths glimmered in the beams of the headlights, and fell to their death.

How easily, Mary thought – fear clutching her heart – death comes to living things. The memory of her little son filled her mind as they drove through the night to meet what might be another tragedy.

At the hospital they were taken to a small waiting room. Within a minute, a doctor came to them. There was no need for him to speak. His face told Mary all. Bertie had gone.

The wayzgoose, begun so gaily, had ended in tragedy. The two buses had drawn up a few miles from Caxley to allow the passengers to have a last drink before closing time. They had to cross a busy road to enter the old coaching inn, famed for its hospitality. Returning to the bus, Bertie and a friend waited some time for a lull in the traffic. It was a busy road, leading to the coast, and despite the late hour the traffic was heavy. At last they made a dash for it, not realizing that a second car was overtaking the one they could see. The latter slowed down to let the two men cross, but the second car could not stop in time. Both men were hurled to the ground, Bertie being dragged some yards before the car stopped.

Despite appalling injuries, he was alive when admitted to hospital, but died within the hour. The organizer of the outing, knowing that Mary was not on the telephone, decided to let the local vicar break the news of the accident.

Mr Partridge and poor Mary returned along the dark lanes to the darker cottage, where he aroused Mrs Berry, told her the terrible story and left her trying to comfort the young widow.

If anyone can succeed, Mr Partridge thought as he drove sadly to his vicarage, she can. But oh, the waste of it all! The wicked waste!

CHAPTER 2

Old Mrs Berry, remembering that dreadful night, shook her head sadly as she washed up her cup and saucer at the sink. The rain still fell in torrents, and a wild wind buffeted the bushes in the garden, sending the leaves tumbling across the grass.

In Caxley it would not be so rough, she hoped. Most of the time her family would be under cover in the shops. But out here, at Shepherds Cross, they always caught the full violence of the weather.

Mrs Berry's cottage was the third one spaced along the road that led to Springbourne. All three cottages were roomy, with large gardens containing gnarled old apple and plum trees. Each cottage possessed ancient hawthorn hedges, supplying sanctuary to dozens of little birds.

An old drovers' path ran at right angles to the cottages, crossing the road by Mrs Berry's house. This gave the hamlet its name, although it was many years since sheep had been driven along that green lane to the great sheep fair at the downland village ten miles distant.

Some thought it a lonely spot, and declared that they 'would go melancholy mad, that they would!' But Mrs Berry, used to remote houses since childhood, was not affected.

She had been brought up in a gamekeeper's cottage in a woodland ride. As a small child she rarely saw anyone strange, except on Sundays, when she attended church with her parents.

She had loved that church, relishing its loftiness, its glowing stained-glass windows and the flowers on the altar. She paid attention to the exhortations of the vicar too, a holy man who truly ministered to his neighbours. From him, as much as from the example of her parents, she learned early to appreciate modesty, courage, and generosity.

When she was old enough to read she deciphered a plaque upon the chancel floor extolling the virtues of a local benefactor, a man of modest means who nevertheless *'was hospitable and charitable all his Days'* and who, at his end, left *'the interest of Forty Pounds to the Poor of the parish forever.'*

It was the next line or two which the girl never forgot, and which influenced her own life. They read:

> *Such were the good effects of*
> *Virtue and Oeconomy.*
> *Read, Grandeur, and Blush*

Certainly, goodness and thrift, combined with a horror of ostentation and boasting, were qualities which Mrs Berry embodied all the days of her life, and her daughters profited by her example.

Mrs Berry left the kitchen and went to sit by the fire in the living room. It was already growing dark, for the sky was thick with storm clouds, and the rain showed no sign of abating.

Water bubbled in the crack of the window frame, and Mrs Berry sighed. It was at times like this one needed a man about the place. Unobtrusively, without complaint, Stanley and then Bertie had attended to such things as draughty windows, wobbly door knobs, squeaking floorboards and the like. Now the women had to cope as best they could, and an old house, about two hundred years of age, certainly needed constant attention to keep it in trim.

Nevertheless, it looked pretty and gay. The Christmas tree, dressed the night before by Jane and Frances – with many squeals of delight – stood on the side table. This table, spangled with stars and tinsel, displayed the Victorian fairy doll, three inches high, which had once adorned the Christmas trees of Mrs Berry's childhood. The doll's tiny wax face was brown with age but still bore that sweet expression which the child had imagined was an angel's.

Sprigs of holly were tucked behind the picture frames, and a spray of mistletoe hung where the oil lamp had once swung from the central beam over the dining table.

Mrs Berry leaned back in her chair and surveyed it all with satisfaction. It looked splendid and there was very little more to be done to the preparations in the kitchen. The turkey was stuffed, the potatoes peeled. The Christmas pudding had been made in November and stood ready on the shelf to be plunged into the steamer tomorrow morning. Mince pies waited in the tin, and a splendid Christmas cake, iced and decorated with robins and holly by Mrs Berry herself, would grace the tea table tomorrow.

There would also be a small Madeira cake, with a delicious sliver of green angelica tucked into its top. The old lady had made that for those who, like herself, could not tackle Christmas cake until three or four hours after Christmas pudding. It had turned out beautifully light, Mrs Berry remembered.

She closed her eyes contentedly, and before long, drifted into a light sleep.

Mrs Berry awoke as the children burst into the room. A cold breeze set the Christmas tree ornaments tinkling and rustled the paper chain, which swung above the door.

The little girls' faces were pink and wet, their bangs stuck to their foreheads and glistened with dampness. Drops fell from the scarlet mackintoshes and their woolly gloves were soaked. But nothing could damp their spirits on this wonderful day, and Mrs Berry forbore to scold them for the mess they were making on the rug.

Mary, struggling with the shopping, called from the kitchen.

'Come out here, you two, and get off those wet things! What a day, Gran! You've never seen anything like Caxley High Street. Worse than Michaelmas Fair! Traffic jams all up the road, and queues in all the shops. The Caxley traders will have a bumper Christmas, mark my words!'

Mrs Berry stirred herself and followed the children into the kitchen to help them undress. Mary was unloading her baskets and carrier bags, rescuing nuts and Brussels sprouts which burst from wet paper bags on to the floor, and trying to take off her own sodden coat and headscarf all at the same time.

'I seem to have spent a mint of money,' she said apologetically, 'and dear knows where it's all gone. We'll have a reckon-up later on, but we were that pushed and hurried about I'll be hard put to it to remember all the prices.'

'No point in worrying,' said Mrs Berry calmly. 'If 'tis gone, 'tis gone. You won't have wasted it, I know that, my girl. Here, let's put on the kettle and make a cup of tea. You must be exhausted.'

'Ah! It's rough out,' agreed Mary, sounding relieved now that she had confessed to forgetting the cost of some of her purchases. 'But it's the rush that takes it out of you. If only that ol' bus came back half an hour later 'twould help. As it is, you have to keep one eye on the town clock all the time you're shopping.'

The little girls were delving into the bags, searching for their own secret shopping.

'Now mind what you're at,' said Mary sharply. 'Take your treasures and put 'em upstairs, and I'll help you pack 'em up when we've had a cup of tea.'

'Don't tell,' wailed Jane. 'It's a secret!'

'A secret!' echoed Frances.

'It still is,' retorted their mother. 'Up you go then, and take the things up carefully. And put on your slippers,' she shouted after them, as they clambered upstairs clutching several small packets against their chests.

'Mad as hatters, they are,' Mary confided to her mother. 'Barmy as March hares – and all because of Christmas!'

'All children are the same,' replied Mrs Berry, pouring boiling water into the teapot, and peering through the silvery steam to make sure it was not overfull. 'You three were as wild as they are, I well remember.' She carried the tray into the living room. 'Could you eat anything?' she asked.

'Not a thing,' said Mary, flopping down, exhausted, into the armchair by the fire, 'and a biscuit will be enough for the girls. They're so excited they won't sleep if they have too much before bedtime.'

'We'll get them upstairs early tonight,' said her mother. 'There are still some presents to pack.'

'We'll be lucky if they go to sleep before nine,' prophesied Mary. 'I heard Jane say she was going to stay awake to see if Father Christmas really does come. She doesn't believe it anymore, you know. I'm positive about that, but she don't let on in case he doesn't come!'

'She's seven,' observed Mrs Berry. 'Can't expect her to believe fairy tales all her life.'

'They've been telling her at school,' said Mary. 'Once they start school they lose all their pretty ways. Frances has only had six months there, but she's too knowing by half.'

The women sipped their tea, listening to the children moving about above them and relishing a few quiet moments on their own.

'They can have a good long time in the bath tonight,' said Mary, thinking ahead, 'then they'll be in trim to go to church with you tomorrow.'

'But wouldn't you like to go?'

'No, Mum. I'll see to the turkey while you're out. The service means more to you than me. Somehow church doesn't seem the same since Bertie went. Pointless, somehow.'

Mrs Berry was too taken aback to comment on this disclosure, and the entry of the children saved her from further conversation on the matter.

Her thoughts were in turmoil as she poured milk into the children's mugs and opened the biscuit tin for their probing fingers.

That unguarded remark of Mary's had confirmed her suspicions. She had watched Mary's growing casualness to religious matters and her increasing absences at church services with real concern. When Stanley died, she had found her greatest consolation in prayer and the teachings of the church. 'Thy Will Be Done,' it said on the arch above the chancel steps, and for old Mrs Berry those words had been both succour, support and reason.

But, with the death of Bertie, Mary had grown hard, and had rejected a God Who allowed such suffering to occur. Mrs Berry could understand the change of heart, but it did not lessen her grief for this daughter who turned her face from the comfort of religious beliefs. Without submission to a divine will, who could be happy? We were too frail to stand and fight alone, but that's what Mary was doing, and why she secretly was so unhappy.

Mrs Berry thrust these thoughts to the back of her mind. It was Christmas Eve, the time for good will to all men, the time to rejoice in the children's pleasure, and to hope that, somehow, the warmth and love of the festival would thaw the frost in Mary's heart.

'Bags not the tap end!' Mrs Berry heard Jane shout an hour later, as the little girls capered naked about the bathroom.

'Mum, she *always* makes me sit the tap end!' complained Frances. 'And the cold tap drips down my back. It's not fair!'

'No grizzling now on Christmas Eve,' said Mary briskly. 'You start the tap end, Frances, and you can change over at halftime. That's fair. You're going to have a nice long bathtime tonight while I'm helping Gran. Plenty of soap, don't forget, and I'll look at your ears when I come back.'

Mrs Berry heard the bath door close, and then open again.

'And stop sucking your facecloth, Frances,' scolded her mother. 'Anyone'd think you're a little baby, instead of a great girl of five.'

The door closed again, and Mary reappeared, smiling.

'They'll be happy for twenty minutes. Just listen to them!'

Two young treble voices, wildly flat, were bellowing 'Away in a manger, no crib for a bed,' to a background of splashes and squeals.

'Did you manage to find some slippers for them?' asked Mrs Berry.

'Yes, Tom's Christine had put them by for me, and I had a quick look while the girls were watching someone try on shoes. There's a lot to be said for knowing people in the shops. They help you out on occasions like this.'

She was rummaging in a deep oilcloth bag as she spoke, and now drew out two boxes. Inside were the slippers. Both were designed to look like rabbits, with shiny black beads for eyes, and silky white whiskers. Jane's pair were blue, and Frances' red. They were Mrs Berry's present to her grandchildren, and she nodded her approval at Mary's choice.

'Very nice, dear, very nice. I'll just tuck a little chocolate bar into each one –'

'There's no need, Mum. This is plenty. You spoil them,' broke in Mary.

'Maybe, but they're going to have the chocolate. Something to wear is a pretty dull Christmas present for a child. I well remember my Aunt Maud – God rest her, poor soul. What a dance she led my Uncle Hubert! She used to give us girls a starched white pinafore every Christmas, and very miserable we thought them.'

She shook her head.

'Ungrateful, weren't we? Now I can see it was a very generous present, as well as being useful; but my old grandad gave us two sugar mice, one pink and one white with long string tails, and they were much more welcome, believe me.'

'Like the tangerine and toffees you and Dad used to tuck in the toe of our stockings.' Mary smiled. 'We always rushed for those first before unpacking the rest. Funny how hungry you are at five in the morning when you're a child!'

'Get me some wrapping paper,' said Mrs Berry briskly, 'and I'll tie them up while those two rascals are safe for ten minutes. They've eyes in the backs of their heads at Christmastime.'

Mary left her mother making two neat parcels. Her wrinkled hands, dappled with brown age spots, were as deft as ever. Spectacles on the end of her nose, the old lady folded the paper this way and that, and tied everything firmly with bright red string.

Mary took the opportunity to smuggle a beautiful pink cyclamen into her own bedroom and hide it behind the curtain on the windowsill. It had cost more than she could really afford, but she had decided to forego a new pair of winter gloves. The old ones could be mended, and who was to notice the much sewn seams in a little place like Shepherds Cross?

She drew the curtains across to hide the plant and to keep out the draught, which was whistling through the cracks of the ancient lattice-paned window. Outside, the wind roared in the branches; a flurry of dead wet leaves flew this way and that as the eddies caught them. The rain slanted down pitilessly, and as a car drove past, the beams of its headlights lit up the shining road where the raindrops spun like silver coins.

She took out from a drawer her own presents for the children. There were two small boxes and two larger ones, and she opened them to have one last look before they were wrapped. In each of the smaller boxes a string of little imitation pearls nestled against a red mock-velvet background. How pretty they would look on the girls' best frocks!

Simple, but good, Mary told herself, with satisfaction. As Mum had said, children wanted something more than everyday presents at Christmas, and the two larger boxes *were* rather dull perhaps.

They held seven handkerchiefs, one for each day of the week, with the appropriate name embroidered in the corner. Sensible, and would teach them how to spell too, thought Mary, putting back the lids.

She was just in time, for at that moment the door burst open and she only had a second in which to thrust the boxes back into the drawer, when two naked cherubs skipped in, still wet with bath water.

'What d'you think –' she began, but was cut short by two vociferous voices in unison.

'The water's all gone. Frances pushed out the plug –'

'I never then!'

'Yes, you did! You know you did! Mum, she wriggled it out with her bottom –'

'Well, she never changed ends, like you said. I only wriggled 'cos the cold tap dripped down my back. I couldn't help it!'

'She done it a-purpose.'

'I never. I told you –'

Mary cut short their protestations.

'You'll catch your deaths. Get on back to the bathroom and start to rub dry. Look at your wet foot marks on the floor! What'll Gran say?'

They began to giggle, eyeing each other.

'Let's go down and frighten her, all bare,' cried Jane.

'Don't you dare now!' said their mother, her voice sharpened by the thought of the slippers being wrapped below.

A little chastened by her tone, the two romped out of the room, jostling together like puppies. Mary heard their squeals of laughter from behind the bathroom door, and smiled at her reflection in the glass.

'"Christmas comes but once a year,"' she quoted aloud. 'Perhaps it's as well!'

She followed her rowdy offspring into the bathroom.

Twenty minutes later the two girls sat barefoot on their wooden stools, one at each side of the fire. On their laps they held steaming bowls of bread and milk, plentifully sprinkled with brown sugar.

'You said we could hang up pillow slips tonight,' remarked Jane, 'instead of stockings.'

'I haven't forgotten. There are two waiting on the banisters for you to put at the end of your bed.'

'Will Father Christmas know?' asked Frances anxiously, her eyes wide with apprehension.

'Of course he will,' said their grandmother robustly. 'He's got plenty of sense. Been doing the job long enough to know what's what.'

Mary glanced at the clock.

'Finish up now. Don't hang it out, you girls. Gran and I've got a lot to do this evening, so you get off to sleep as quick as you can.'

'I'm staying awake till he comes,' said Jane firmly.

'Me too,' echoed Frances, scooping the last drop of milk from the bowl.

They went to kiss their grandmother. She held their soft faces against hers, relishing the sweet smell of soap and milk. How dear these two small mortals were!

'The sooner you get to sleep, the sooner the morning will come,' she told them.

She watched them as, followed by Mary, they tumbled up the staircase that opened from the room.

'I *shall* stay awake!' protested Jane. 'I shan't close my eyes, not for *one minute!* I promise you!'

Mrs Berry smiled to herself as she put another log on the fire. She had heard that tale many times before. If she were a betting woman she would lay a wager that those two would be fast asleep within the hour!

But, for once, Mrs Berry was wrong.

CHAPTER 3

Upstairs, in the double bed, the two little girls pulled the clothes to their chins and continued their day-long conversation.

A nightlight, secure in a saucer on the dressing table, sent great shadows bowing and bending across the sloping ceiling, for the room was crisscrossed with draughts on this wild night from the ill-fitting window and door. Sometimes the brave little flame bent in a sudden blow from the cold air, as a crocus does in a gust of wind, but always it righted itself, continuing to give out its comforting light to the young children.

'Shall I tell you why I'm going to stay awake all night?' asked Jane.

'Yes.'

'Promise to do what I tell you?'

'Yes.'

'Promise *faithfully*? See my finger wet and dry? Cross your heart? *Everything?*'

'Everything,' agreed Frances equably. Her eyelids were beginning to droop already. Left alone, free from the vehemence of her sister, she would have fallen asleep within a minute.

'Then eat your pillow,' demanded Jane.

Frances was hauled back roughly from the rocking sea of sleep.

'You know I can't!' she protested.

'You promised,' said Jane.

'Well, I unpromise,' declared Frances. 'I can't eat a pillow, and anyway what would Mum say?'

'Then I shan't tell you what I was going to.'

'I don't care,' replied Frances untruthfully.

Jane, enraged by such lack of response and such wanton breaking of solemn vows, bounced over on to her side, her back to Frances.

'It was about Father Christmas,' she said hotly, 'but I'm not telling you now.'

'He'll come,' said Frances drowsily.

This confidence annoyed Jane still further.

'Maybe he won't then! Tom Williams says there isn't a Father Christmas. That's why I'm going to stay awake. To see. So there!'

Through the veils of sleep which were fast enmeshing her, Frances pondered upon this new problem. Tom Williams was a big boy, ten years old at least. What's more, he was a sort of cousin. He should know what he was talking about. Nevertheless . . .

'Tom Williams don't always speak the truth,' answered Frances. In some ways, she was a wiser child than her sister.

Jane gave an impatient snort.

'Besides,' said Frances, following up her point, 'our teacher said he'd come. She don't tell lies. Nor Mum, nor Gran.'

These were powerful allies, and Jane was conscious that Frances had some support.

'Grownups hang together,' said Jane darkly. 'Don't forget we saw *two* Father Christmases this afternoon in Caxley. What about that then?'

'They was men dressed up,' replied Frances stolidly. 'Only *pretend* Father Christmases. It don't mean there isn't a real one as 'll come tonight.'

A huge yawn caught her unawares.

'You stay awake if you want to,' she murmured, turning her head into the delicious warmth of the uneaten pillow. 'I'm going to sleep.'

Secure in her faith, she was asleep in five minutes, but Jane, full of doubts and resentful of her sister's serenity, threw her arms above her head, and, gripping the rails of the brass bedstead, grimly began her vigil. Tonight she would learn the truth!

Downstairs, the two women assembled the last few presents that needed wrapping on the big table.

They made a motley collection. There were three or four pieces of basketwork made by Mary, who was neat with her fingers, and these she eyed doubtfully.

'Can't see myself ever making a tidy parcel of these flower holders,' she remarked. 'D'you think just a Christmas tag tied on would be all right?'

Mrs Berry surveyed the hanging baskets thought-fully.

'Well, it always looks a bit slapdash, I feel, to hand over something unwrapped. Looks as though you can't be bothered –'

'I can't,' said Mary laconically.

'But I see your point. We'd make a proper pig's ear of the wrapping paper trying to cover those. You're right, my girl. Just a tag.'

Mary sat down thankfully and drew the packet of tags towards her. The presents were destined for neighbours, and the tags seemed remarkably juvenile for the elderly couples who were going to receive the baskets. Father Christmas waved from a chimney pot, a golliwog danced a jig, two pixies bore a Christmas tree, and a cat carried a Christmas pudding. Only two tags measured up to Mary's requirements, a row of bells on one and a red candle on the other. Ah well, she told herself, someone must make do with the pixies or the cat, and when you came to think of it the tags would be on the back of the fire this time tomorrow, so why worry? She wrote diligently.

Outside the wind still screamed, rattling the window, and making the back door thump in its frame. The curtains stirred in the onslaught, and now and again a little puff of smoke came into the room from the log fire, as the wind eddied round the chimney pot.

Mrs Berry looked up from the jar of honey she was wrapping.

'I'll go and see if the rain's blowing in under that door at the back.'

She went out, causing a draught that rustled the

wrapping paper and blew two of Mary's tags to the floor. Mrs Berry was gone for some minutes, and returned red-faced from stooping.

'A puddle a good yard wide,' she puffed. 'I've left that old towel stuffed up against the crack. We'll have to get a new sill put on that threshold, Mary. It's times like this we miss our menfolk.'

Mary nodded, not trusting herself to speak. Hot tears pricked her eyes, but she bent lower to her task, so that her mother should not see them. How was it, she wondered, that she could keep calm and talk about her loss, quite in control of her feelings, for nine tenths of the time, and yet a chance remark, like this one, pierced her armour so cruelly? Poor Gran! If only she knew! Better, of course, that she did not. She would never forgive herself if she thought she had caused pain.

Unaware of the turmoil in her daughter's mind, Mrs Berry turned her attention to a round tin of shortbread.

"Pon my word,' she remarked. 'I never learn! After all these years, you'd think I'd know better than to pick a round tin instead of a square 'un. I'll let you tackle this, Mary. It's for Margaret and Mary Waters. They're good to us all through the year, taking messages and traipsing round with the parish magazine in all weathers.'

Mary reached across for the tin, then checked. The eyes of the two women met questioningly. Above the sound of the gale outside they had heard the metallic clink of their letter box.

'I'll go,' said Mary.

An envelope lay on the damp mat. She opened the door, letting in a rush of wind and rain and a few sodden leaves. There was no one to be seen, but in

the distance Mary thought she could see the bobbing
light of a flashlight. To shout would have been useless. To follow, in her slippers, idiotic. She pushed
the door shut against the onslaught, and returned to
the light with the envelope.

'For you, Mum,' she said, handing over the glistening packet.

Mrs Berry withdrew a Christmas card, bright with
robins and frosted leaves, and two embroidered
white handkerchiefs.

'From Mrs Burton,' said Mrs Berry wonderingly.
'Now, who'd have thought it? Never exchanged
presents before, have we? What makes her do a thing
like this, I wonder? And turning out too, on such a
night. Dear soul, she shouldn't have done it. She's
little enough to spare as it is.'

'You did feed her cat and chickens for her while she was away last summer,' said Mary. 'Perhaps that's why.'

'That's only acting neighbourly,' protested Mrs Berry. 'No call for her to spend money on us.'

'Given her pleasure, I don't doubt,' answered Mary. 'The thing is, do we give her something back? And, if so, what?'

It was a knotty problem. Their eyes ranged over the presents before them, already allotted.

'We'll have to find *something*,' said Mrs Berry firmly. 'What about that box of soap upstairs?'

'People are funny about soap,' said Mary. 'Might think it's a hint, you know. She's none too fond of washing, nice old thing though she is.'

They racked their brains in silence.

'Half a pound of tea?' suggested Mrs Berry at last.

'Looks like charity,' replied Mary.

'Well, I wouldn't say no to a nice packet of tea,' said Mrs Berry with spirit. 'What about one of our new tea towels then?'

'Cost too much,' said Mary. 'She'd mind about that.'

'I give up then,' said Mrs Berry. 'You think of something. I must say these last-minute surprises are all very fine, but they do put you to some thinking.'

She tied a final knot round the honey pot and rose to her feet again.

'Talking of tea, what about a cup?'

'Lovely,' said Mary.

'Shall I cut us a sandwich?'

'Not for me. Just a cup of tea.'

The old lady went out, and Mary could hear the

clattering of cups and saucers, and the welcome tinkle of teaspoons. Suddenly, she felt inexpressibly tired. She longed to put her head down among the litter on the table and fall asleep. Sometimes she thought Christmas was more trouble than it was worth. All the fuss and flurry, then an empty purse just as the January bills came in. If only she had her mother's outlook! She still truly loved Christmas. She. truly celebrated the birth of that God who walked beside her every hour of the day. She truly loved her neighbour – even that dratted Mrs Burton, who was innocently putting them to such trouble.

Mrs Berry returned with the round tin tray bearing the cups and saucers and the homely brown teapot clad in a knitted tea cosy. Her face had a triumphant smile.

'I've thought of something. A bottle of my blackcurrant wine. How's that? She can use it for her cough, if she don't like it for anything better. What say?'

'Perfect!' said Mary. In agreement at last, they sipped their tea thankfully.

Still awake upstairs, Jane heard the chinking of china and the voices of her mother and grandmother. Beside her, Frances snored lightly, her pink mouth slightly ajar, her lashes making dark crescents against her rosy cheeks.

Jane's vigil seemed lonelier and bleaker every minute. What's more, she was hungry, she discovered. The thought of the blue biscuit tin, no doubt standing by the teacups below, caused her stomach to rumble. Cautiously, she slid her skinny legs out of bed, took a swift glance at the two empty pillowcases draped expectantly one each end of the brass bed rail, and crept to the door.

The wind was making so much noise that no one heard the latch click, or the footsteps on the stairs. The child opened the bottom door, which led directly into the living room, and stood blinking in the light like a little owl caught in the sunshine.

'Mercy me!' gasped Mrs Berry, putting down her cup with a clatter. 'What a start you gave me, child!'

'Jane!' cried her mother. 'What on earth are you doing down here?' Her voice was unusually sharp. Surprised and startled, she could have shaken the child in her exasperation.

'I'm hungry,' whispered Jane, conscious of her un-popularity.

'You had a good supper,' said Mary shortly. 'Time you was asleep.'

'Let her come by the fire for a minute,' pleaded Mrs Berry. 'Shut that door, my dear. The draught fairly cuts through us. Want a cup of tea, and a biscuit?'

The child's face lit up.

'Shall I fetch a cup?'

'Not with those bare feet,' said Mary. 'I'll get your mug, and then you go straight back to bed as soon as you're finished. Your gran's too good to you.'

She hurried kitchenwards, and the child sat on the rag rug smiling at the flames licking the log. It was snug down here. It was always snug with Gran.

She put a hand on the old lady's knee.

'Mum's cross,' she whispered.

'She's tired. Done a lot today, and you know you should really be abed, giving her a break.'

They always hang together, these grownups, thought Jane rebelliously; but she took the mug of weak tea gratefully, and the top biscuit from the tin when it was offered, even though it was a Rich Tea and she knew there were Ginger Nuts further down.

'Is Frances asleep?' asked Mary.

'Yes. I couldn't get off.'

'You told me you didn't intend to,' replied her mother. 'Trying to see Father Christmas, silly girl. As though he'll come if you're awake! The sooner you're asleep the sooner he'll come!'

Torn with doubts, the child looked swiftly up into her grandmother's face. It told her nothing. The familiar kind smile played around the lips. The eyes looked down at her as comfortingly as ever.

'Your mother's right. Drink up your tea, and then snuggle back into bed. I'll come and tuck you up this time.'

Jane tilted her mug, put the last fragment of biscuit into her mouth, and scrambled to her feet.

'Whose presents are those?' she said, suddenly aware of the parcels on the table.

'Not yours,' said Mary.

'Neighbours',' said her grandmother in the same breath. 'You shall take some round for us tomorrow. And I want you to carry a bottle of wine very carefully to Mrs Burton. Can you do it, do you think?'

The child nodded, hesitated before her mother, then kissed her warmly on the cheek.

'You hussy!' said Mary, but her voice was soft, and the child saw that she was forgiven. Content at last, she followed her grandmother's bulk up the narrow stairs.

The flame of the night light was burning low in

the little hollow of its wax. The shadows wavered about the room as the old woman and the child moved towards the bed.

'Now, no staying awake, mind,' whispered Gran, in a voice that brooked no argument. 'I don't know who's been stuffing your head with nonsense, but you can forget it. Get off to sleep, like Frances there. You'll see Father Christmas has been, as soon as you wake up.'

She kissed the child, and tucked in the bedclothes tightly.

Jane listened to her grandmother's footsteps descending the creaking stairs, sighed for her lost intentions, and fell, almost instantly, into a deep sleep.

CHAPTER 4

'My! That was a lucky escape,' said Mrs Berry. 'Good thing we hadn't got out those pillowcases!'

Two pillowcases, identical to those hanging limply upstairs, had been hidden behind the couch in the cottage parlour for the last two days. Most of the presents were already in them. There were a doll for each, beautifully dressed in handsewn clothes, joint presents from Mary and her mother; a game of Ludo for Frances and Snakes and Ladders for Jane; and a jigsaw puzzle apiece. All should provide plenty of future pleasure.

The American aunt had sent two little cardigans, pale pink and edged with silver trimming – far more glamorous than anything to be found in the Caxley shops. The less well-off aunt at Taunton had sent bath salts for both, which, Mary knew, would enchant the little girls. There were also gifts from kind neighbours – a box of beads, a toy shop (complete with tiny metal scales), and several tins of sweets, mint humbugs and homemade toffee among them.

A stocking, waiting to be filled with small knickknacks, lay across each pillowcase. As soon as the children were safely asleep, the plan had been to substitute the full pillowcases for the empty ones.

'I thought she might reappear,' admitted Mary. 'She's twigged, you know, about Father Christmas. Some of the children at school have let it out.'

'She won't come down again, I'm certain,' replied Mrs Berry comfortingly. 'Let's fill up the stockings, shall we? We can put the last-minute odds and ends in when we carry up the pillowcases.'

Mary nodded agreement and went to the parlour, returning with the limp stockings. They were a pair of red and white striped woollen ones, once the property of the vicar's aunt, and reputedly kept for skating and skiing in her young days. Mary had bought them at a jumble sale, and each Christmas since they had appeared to delight the little girls.

From the dresser drawer, Mrs Berry collected the store of small treasures that had been hidden there for the last week or so. A few wrapped sweets, a curly stick of barley sugar, a comb, a tiny pencil and pad, a brooch and a handkerchief followed the tangerines that stuffed the toe of each stocking. Then, almost guiltily, Mrs Berry produced the final touch – too small wooden Dutch dolls.

'Saw them in the market at Caxley,' she said, 'and couldn't resist them, Mary. They reminded me of a family of Dutch dolls I had at their age. They can amuse themselves dressing them up.'

The dolls were tucked at the top, their shiny black heads and stiff wooden arms sticking out attractively. The two women gazed at their handiwork with satisfaction.

'Well, that's that!' said Mrs Berry. 'I'm just going to clear away this tray and tidy up in the kitchen, and I shan't be long out of bed.'

'I'll wait till I'm sure those two scallywags are really asleep,' answered Mary. 'I wouldn't put it past our Jane to pretend, you know. She's stubborn when she wants to be, and she's real set on finding out who brings the presents.'

The hands of the clock on the mantelpiece stood at ten o'clock. How the evening had flown! Mary tidied the table, listening to the gale outside, and the sound of her mother singing in the kitchen.

She suddenly remembered her own small presents upstairs still unwrapped and crept aloft to fetch them. The door of the girls' room was ajar. She tiptoed in and looked down upon the sleeping pair. It seemed impossible that either of them could be feigning sleep, so rhythmically were they breathing. What angels they looked!

She made her way downstairs and swiftly wrapped up the necklaces and handkerchiefs. The very last, she thought thankfully! Just a tag for Mum's cyclamen, and I can write that and tie it on when I go to bed.

She selected the prettiest tag she could find, and slipped it into her skirt pocket to take upstairs.

Mrs Berry reappeared, carrying the glass of water that she took to her bedroom every night.

'I'll be off then, my dear. Don't stay up too long. You must be tired.'

She bent to kiss her daughter.

'The girls have gone off, I think, but I'll give them another ten minutes to make sure.'

'See you in the morning, then, Mary,' said the old lady, mounting the stairs.

Mary raked the hot ashes from the fire and swept up the hearth. She fetched the two bulging pillowcases and put the stockings on top of them. Then she sat in the old armchair and let exhaustion flood through her. Bone-tired, she confessed to herself. Bone-tired!

Above her she could hear the creaking of the floor-boards as her mother moved about, then a cry and hasty footsteps coming down the stairs.

The door flew open and Mrs Berry, clad in her flannel nightgown, stood, wild eyed, on the threshold.

'Mum, what's the matter?' cried Mary, starting to her feet.

'A mouse!' gasped Mrs Berry, shuddering uncontrollably. 'There's a mouse in my bedroom!'

The two women gazed at each other, horror struck. Mary's heart sank rapidly, but she spoke decisively.

'Here, you come by the fire, and let's shut that door. The girls will be waking up.'

She pushed up the armchair she had just vacated and Mrs Berry, still shuddering, sat down thankfully.

'You'll catch your death,' said Mary, raking a few bright embers together and dropping one or two shreds of dry bark from the hearth on to the dying fire. 'You ought to have put on your dressing gown.'

'I'm not going up there to fetch it!' stated Mrs Berry flatly. 'I know I'm a fool, but I just can't abide mice.'

'I'll fetch it,' said Mary, 'and I'll set the mousetrap too while I'm there. Where did it go?'

Mrs Berry shivered afresh.

'It ran under the bed, horrible little thing! You should've seen its tail, Mary! A good three inches long! It made me cry out, seeing it skedaddle like that.'

'I heard you,' said Mary, making for the kitchen to get the mousetrap.

Mrs Berry drew nearer to the fire, tucking her voluminous nightgown round her bare legs. A cruel draught whistled in from the passage, but nothing would draw her from the safety of the armchair. Who knows how many more mice might be at large on a night like this?

Mary, her mouth set in a determined line, re-appeared with the mousetrap and went quietly up-stairs. She returned in a moment, carrying her mother's dressing gown and slippers.

'Now you wrap up,' she said coaxingly, as if she were addressing one of her little daughters. 'We'll soon catch that old mouse for you.'

'I'm ashamed to be so afeared of a little creature,' confessed Mrs Berry, 'but there it is. They give me the horrors, mice do, and rats even worse. Don't ask me why!'

Mary knew from experience this terror of her mother's. She confronted other hazards of country life with calm courage. Spiders, caterpillars, bulls in fields, adders on the heath, any animals in pain or fury found old Mrs Berry completely undaunted. Mary could clearly remember her mother dealing with a dog that had been run over and writhed, demented with pain, not far from their cottage door. It had savaged two would-be helpers, and a few distressed onlookers were wondering what to do next when Mrs Berry approached and calmed the animal in a way that had seemed miraculous. But a mouse sent her flying, and Mary knew, as she found some wood to replenish the fire, that nothing would persuade her mother back to the bedroom until the intruder had been dispatched.

She settled herself in the other armchair, resigned to another twenty minutes or more of waiting. She longed desperately for her bed, but could not relax until her mother was comfortably settled. She listened for sounds from above – the click of the mousetrap that would release her from her vigil, or the noise of the children waking and rummaging for the pillowcases, wailing at the nonappearance of Father Christmas.

But above the noise of the storm outside, it was difficult to hear anything clearly upstairs. She pushed the two telltale pillowcases under the table, so that they were hidden from the eyes of any child who might enter unannounced, and leaned back with her eyes closed.

Invariably, Bertie's dear face drifted before her when she closed her eyes, but now, to her surprise and shame, another man's face smiled at her. It was the face of one of Bertie's workmates. He too had been one of the party on that tragic wayzgoose, and had written to Mary and her mother soon after the accident. She had known him from childhood. Rather a milksop, most people said of Ray Bullen, but Mary liked his gentle ways and thought none the less of him because he had remained a bachelor.

'Some are the marrying sort, and some aren't,' she had replied once to the village gossip who had been speculating upon Ray's future. Mary was all too conscious of the desire of busybodies to find her a husband in the months after Bertie's death. They got short shrift from Mary, and interest waned before long.

'Too sharp tongued by half,' said those who had been lashed by it. 'No man in his senses would take her on, with them two girls too.'

Here they were wrong. One or two men had paid attention to Mary, and would have welcomed some advances on her side. But none were forthcoming. Truth to tell, Mary was in such a state of numbed shock for so long that very little affected her.

But Ray's letter of condolence had been kept. There was something unusually warm and comforting in the simple words. Here was true sympathy. It was the only letter that had caused Mary to weep and, weeping, to find relief.

She saw Ray very seldom, for their ways did not cross. But that afternoon in Caxley he had been at the bus stop when she arrived laden with baskets and anxious about the little girls amidst the Christmas traffic. He had taken charge of them all so easily and naturally – seeing them on to the bus, disposing of the parcels, smiling at the children and wishing them all well at Christmas – that it was not until she was halfway to Shepherds Cross that Mary realized that he had somehow contrived to give the little girls a shilling each. Also, she realized with a pang, he must have missed his own bus, which went out about the same time as theirs.

She supposed, leaning back now in the armchair, that her extreme tiredness had brought his face before her tonight. It was not a handsome face, to be sure, but it was kind and gentle, and, from all she heard, Ray Bullen had both those qualities as well as strong principles. He was a Quaker, she knew, and she remembered a little passage about Quakers from the library book she was reading. Something about them 'making the best chocolate and being very thoughtful and wealthy and good.' It had amused her at the time, and though Ray Bullen could never be said to be wealthy, he was certainly thoughtful and good.

She became conscious of her mother's voice, garrulous in her nervousness.

'It's funny how you can sense them when you're frightened of them. Not that I had any premonition tonight, I was too busy thinking about getting those pillowcases safely upstairs. But I well remember helping my aunt clear out her scullery when I was a child. No older than Frances, I was then, and she asked me to lift a little old keg she kept her flour in. And, do you know, I began to tremble, and I told her I just couldn't do it. "There's a mouse in there!" I told her.

'She was so wild. "Rubbish!" she stormed. She was a quick-tempered woman, red haired and plump, and couldn't bear to be crossed. "Pick it up at once!"

'And so I did. And when I looked inside, there *was* a mouse, dead as a doornail and smelling to high heaven! I dropped that double quick, you can be sure, and it rolled against a bottle of cider and smashed it to smithereens. Not that I waited to see it happen. I was down at the end of the garden, in the privy with the door bolted. She couldn't get at me there!'

Mary had heard the tale many times, but would not have dreamed of reminding her mother of the fact. It was her mother's way, she realized, of apologizing for the trouble she was causing.

Mrs Berry hated to be a nuisance, and now, with Mary so near to complete exhaustion, she was being the biggest nuisance possible, the old lady told herself guiltily. Why must that dratted mouse arrive in her bedroom on Christmas Eve?

In the silence that had fallen there was the unmistakeable click of a mousetrap. Mary leaped to her feet.

'Thank God!' said Mrs Berry in all seriousness. Panic seized her once more. 'Don't let me see it, Mary, will you? I can't bear to see their tails hanging down.'

'I'll bring the whole thing down in the wastepaper basket,' promised Mary.

But when she returned to the apprehensive old lady waiting below, she had nothing in her hand.

'He took a nibble and then got away,' she said. 'We'll have to wait a bit longer. I've set it a mite finer this time.'

'I wish you had a braver mother,' said Mrs Berry forlornly. Mary smiled at her, and her mother's heart turned over. The girl looked ten years younger when she smiled. She didn't smile enough, that was the trouble. Time she got over Bertie's loss. There was a time for grieving, and a time to stop grieving. After all, she was still young and, smiling as she was now, very pretty too.

Conversation lapsed, and the two tired women listened to the little intimate domestic noises of the house, the whispering of the flames, the hiss of a damp log, the rattle of the loose-fitting window. Outside, the rain fell down pitilessly. Mrs Berry wondered if the rolled-up towel was stemming the flood at the back door but was too tired to go and see.

She must have dozed, for when she looked at the clock it was almost eleven. Mary was sitting forward in her chair, eyes fixed dreamily on the fire, miles away from Shepherds Cross.

She stirred as her mother sat up.

'I'll go and see if we've had any luck.'

Up the stairs she tiptoed once more, and returned almost immediately. She looked deathly pale with tiredness, and Mrs Berry's heart was moved.

'Still empty. He's a fly one, that mouse. What shall we do?'

Mrs Berry took charge with a flash of her old energy and spirit.

'You're going to bed, my girl. You're about done in, I can see. I'll stay down here for the night, for go up to that bedroom I simply cannot do!'

'But, Mum, it's such a beast of a night! You'd be better off in bed. Just wake me if the trap springs and I'll come and see to it. It's no bother, honest.'

'No, Mary, you've done more than enough, and tomorrow's a busy day. I'll be all right here in the armchair. 'Tisn't the first time I've slept downstairs, and the storm don't trouble me.'

Mary looked doubtfully at the old lady but could see that her mind was made up.

'All right then, Mum. I'll go and fetch your eiderdown and pillow, and see you've got enough firing handy.'

Yet again she mounted the stairs, while Mrs Berry made up the fire and bravely went to have a quick look at the towel by the back door. No more water had seeped in, so presumably the defenses were doing their work satisfactorily. She returned to the snug living room to find Mary plumping up the pillow.

'Now, you're sure you're all right?' she asked anxiously. 'If I hear that trap go off before I get to sleep, shall I call you?'

'No, my dear. You'll be asleep as soon as your head hits the pillow tonight. I can see that. I shall settle here and be perfectly happy.'

Mary retrieved the pillowcases, kissed her mother's forehead, and went to the staircase for the last time that night.

'Sleep well,' she said, smiling at her mother, who by now was wrapped in the eiderdown. 'You look as snug as a bug in a rug, as the children say.'

'Good night, Mary. You're a good girl,' said her mother, watching the door close behind her daughter.

Nearly half-past eleven, thought Mrs Berry. What a time to go to bed! Ten o'clock was considered quite late enough for the early risers of Shepherds Cross.

She struggled from her wrappings to turn off the light and to put a little small coal on the back of the fire. The room was very pretty and cosy by the flickering firelight. There was no sound from upstairs. All three of them, thought Mrs Berry, would be asleep by now, and that wretched mouse still making free in her own bedroom, no doubt.

Ah well, she was safe enough down here, and there was something very companionable about a fire in the room when you were settling down for the night.

She turned her head into the feather-filled pillow. Outside the storm still raged and she could hear the rain drumming relentlessly upon the roof and the road. It made her own comfort doubly satisfying.

God pity all poor travellers on a night like this, thought Mrs Berry, pulling up the eiderdown. 'There's one thing: I shan't be awake long, storm or no storm.'

She sighed contentedly and composed herself for slumber.

CHAPTER 5

But, tired though she was, Mrs Berry could not get
to sleep. Perhaps it was the horrid shock of the
mouse, or the unusual bustle of Christmas that had
overtired her. Whatever the reason, the old lady
found herself gazing at the rosy reflection of the fire
on the ceiling, her mind drifting from one inconse-
quent subject to the next.

The bubbling of rain forcing its way through the
crack of the window reminded her of the more
ominous threat at the back door. Well, she told herself, that towel was standing up to the onslaught
when she looked a short while ago. It must just take
its chance. In weather like this, usual precautions
were not enough. Stanley would have known what
to do. A rolled up towel wouldn't have been good
enough for him! Some sturdy carpentry would have
made sure that the back door was completely
weather-proof.

Mrs Berry sighed and thought wistfully of their
manless state. Two good husbands gone, and no
sons growing up to take their place in the household!
It seemed hard, but the ways of God were inscrut-
able and who was to say why He had taken them
first?

She thought of her first meeting with Stanley,
when she was nineteen and he two years older.
She had been in service then at the vicarage. Her

employer was a predecessor of Mr Partridge's, a bachelor who held the living of Fairacre for many years.
He was a vague, saintly man, a great Hebrew scholar
who had written a number of learned commentaries
on the minor prophets of the Old Testament. His
parishioners were proud of his scholarship but, between themselves, admitted that he was 'only ninepence
in the shilling' when it came to practical affairs.

Nevertheless, the vicarage was well run by a
motherly old body who had once been nurse to a
large family living in a castle in the next county.
This training stood her in good stead when she took
over the post of housekeeper to the vicar of Fairacre.
She was methodical, energetic and abundantly kind.
When a vacancy occurred for a young maid at the
vicarage, Mrs Berry's parents thought she would be
extremely lucky to start work in such pleasant surroundings. They applied for the post for their daughter, then aged thirteen.

Despite her lonely upbringing in the gamekeeper's
cottage, Amelia Scott, as she was then, was a friendly
child, anxious to help and blessed with plenty of
common sense. The housekeeper realized her worth,
and trained her well, letting her help in the kitchen
as well as learning the secrets of keeping the rest of
the establishment sweet and clean.

She thrived under the old lady's tuition, and
learned by her example to respect the sterling
qualities of her employer. He was always ready to
help his neighbours, putting aside his papers to assist
anyone in trouble, and welcoming all – even the
malodorous vagrants who 'took advantage of him',
according to the housekeeper – into his study to give
them refreshment of body and spirit.

One bright June morning, when the dew sparkled on the roses, Amelia heard the chinking of metal on stone, and leaned out of the bedroom window to see two men at work on one of the buttresses of St Patrick's church. The noise continued all the morning, and as the sun rose in the blue arc of a cloudless sky, she wondered if the master would send her across with a jug of cider to wash down the men's dinners, as he often did. Then she remembered that he was out visiting at the other end of the parish. The housekeeper too was out on an errand. She was choosing the two plumpest young fowls, now running about in a neighbour's chicken run, for the Sunday meal.

Amelia was helping Bertha, the senior housemaid, to clean out the attics when they heard the ringing of the back-door bell.

'You run and see to that,' said Bertha, her arms full of derelict pillows. 'I'll carry on here.'

Amelia sped downstairs through the shadows and sunlight that streaked the faded blue carpet, and opened the back door.

A young man, with thick brown hair and very bright dark eyes, smiled at her apologetically.

He held his left hand, which was heavily swathed in a red spotted handkerchief, in his right one, and dark stains showed that he was bleeding profusely.

'Been a bit clumsy,' he said. 'My tool slipped.'

'Come in,' said Amelia, very conscious that she was alone to cope with this emergency. She led the way to the scullery and directed the young man to the shallow slate sink.

'Put your hand in that bowl,' she told him, 'and I'll pump some water. 'It's very pure. We've got one of the deepest wells in the parish.'

It was certainly a nasty gash, and the pure water, so warmly recommended by Amelia, was soon cloudy with blood.

'Keep swilling it around,' directed Amelia, quite enjoying her command of the situation, 'while I get a bit of rag to bandage it.'

'There's no need miss,' protested the young man. 'It's stopping. Look!'

He held out the finger, but even as he did so, the blood began to well again. Amelia took one look and went to the bandage drawer in the kitchen dresser. Here, old pieces of linen sheeting were kept for just such an emergency, and the housekeeper's pot of homemade salve stood permanently on the shelf above.

No one quite knew what the ingredients of this

cure-all were, for the recipe's secret was jealously guarded, but goose grease played a large part in it, along with certain herbs that the old lady gathered from the hedgerows. During the few years of Amelia's residence at the vicarage she had seen this salve used for a variety of ailments, from chilblains to the vicar's shaving rash, and always with good results.

She returned now with the linen and the pot of ointment. The young man still smiled, and Amelia smiled back.

'Let me wrap it up,' she said. 'Let's put some of this stuff on first.'

'What's in it?'

'Nothin' to hurt you.' Amelia assured him. 'It's good for everything. Cured some spots I had on my chin quicker 'n lightning.'

'I don't believe you ever had spots,' said the young man gallantly. He held out the wounded finger, and Amelia twisted the strip round and round deftly, cutting the end in two to make a neat bow.

'There,' she said with pride, 'now you'll be more comfortable.'

'Thank you, miss. You've been very kind.'

He picked up the bloodied handkerchief.

'Leave that here,' said Amelia, 'and I'll wash it for you.'

'No call to trouble you with that,' said the young man. 'My ma will wash it when I get back.'

'Blood stains need soaking in cold water,' Amelia told him,' 'and the sooner the better. I'll put it to soak now, then wash it out.'

'Well, thank you. We're working on the church for the rest of the week. Can I call in tomorrow to get it?'

Amelia felt a glow of pleasure at the thought of seeing him again, so soon. She liked his thick hair, his quick eyes, and his well-tanned skin – a proper nut-brown man, and polite too. Amelia looked at him with approval.

'I'll be here,' she promised.

'My name's Berry,' said the young man. 'Stanley Berry. What's yours?'

'Amelia Scott.'

'Well, thank you, Amelia, for a real good job. I must be getting back to work or I'll get sacked.'

She watched him cross the garden in the shimmering heat, the white bandage vivid against the brown background of his skin and clothes. He paused in the gateway leading to the churchyard, waving to her.

Delighted, she waved back.

'You've taken your time,' grumbled Bertha, when she returned to the attic. She looked at Amelia's radiant face shrewdly.

'Who'd you see down there? Prince Charming?'

Amelia forbore to answer, but thought that Bertha seemed to have guessed correctly.

The next morning the young man called to collect his handkerchief. Amelia had washed and ironed it with extreme care, and had put it carefully on the corner of the dresser to await its owner.

He carried a bunch of pink roses, and at the sight of them Amelia felt suddenly shy.

'You shouldn't have bothered,' she began, but the young man hastily put her at ease.

'My ma sent them, to thank you for what you did,

and for washing the handkerchief. She said you're quite right. She'd have had the devil's own job to get out the stain if I'd left it till evening.'

Amelia took the bunch and smelled them rapturously.

'Please to thank her for them. They're lovely. I'll put them in my room.'

Stanley gave her a devastating smile again.

'I picked them,' he said gently.

'Then, thank you too,' said Amelia, handing over the handkerchief.

They stood in silence for a moment, gazing at each other, loath to break the spell of this magic moment.

'Best be going,' said Stanley, at length. He gave a gusty sigh, which raised Amelia's spirits considerably, and set off, stuffing the handkerchief in his pocket. He had not gone more than a few steps when he halted and turned.

'Can I come again, Amelia?'

'Please,' said Amelia, with rather more fervor than a well-bred young lady should have shown. But then Amelia always spoke her mind.

There was no looking back, no hesitation, no lovers' quarrels. From that first meeting they trod a smooth, blissfully happy path of courtship. They were both even-tempered, considerate people, having much the same background and, most important of all, the same sense of fun. There were no family difficulties, and the wedding took place on a spring day as sunny as that on which they had first met.

They lived for the first few years at Beech Green,

in a small cottage thatched by Dolly Clare's father, who was one of their neighbours. The first two girls were born there, and then the house at Shepherds Cross was advertised to let. It was considerably bigger than their first house, and although it meant a longer cycle ride for Stanley, this did not deter him.

Here Mary was born. They had hoped for a boy this time, but the baby was so pretty and good that the accident of her sex was speedily forgotten.

Amelia and Stanley were true homemakers. Amelia's early training at the vicarage had given her many skills. She could make frocks for the children, curtains, bedspreads, and rag rugs as competently as she could make a cottage pie or a round of short-bread. The house always looked as bright as a new pin, and Stanley saw to it that any stonework or woodwork was in good repair. They shared the gardening and it was Mrs Berry's pride that they never needed to buy a vegetable.

The longing for a son had never left Amelia. She liked a man about the place, and it was doubly grievous when Stanley died so suddenly. She lost not only her lover and husband, but the comfort of all that a shared life meant.

Mary's Bertie brought back to the cottage the feeling of comfort and reliability. The birth of her grandson had meant more to Mrs Berry than she cared to admit. It was the continuance of male protection that subconsciously she needed. The baby's early death was something she mourned as deeply as Mary and Bertie had.

A piece of wood fell from the fire, and Mrs Berry stirred herself to reach for the tongs and replace it.

Not yet midnight! She seemed to have been lying there for hours, dreaming of times passed.

Poor Stanley, poor Bertie, poor baby! But what a blessing the two little girls were! Mary knew how to bring up children. Plenty of fun, but no nonsense when it came to doing as they were told. Say what you will, thought old Mrs Berry, it didn't do people any harm to have a little discipline. You could cosset them too much, and give in to their every whim, and what happiness did that bring?

She remembered neighbours in the early days of her marriage at Beech Garden. They were an elderly pair when their first child arrived, a pale sickly little fellow called, much to the ribaldry of some of the Beech Green folk, Clarence.

The baby was only put out into the garden on the warmest days, and then he was so swaddled in clothes that this normally waxen complexion was beaded with perspiration. The doctor harangued the doting mother; friends and neighbours, genuinely concerned for the child's health, proffered advice. Nothing was of any avail. Clarence continued to be smothered with love.

Not surprisingly, he was late in walking and talking. When he was at the toddling stage, his mother knitted him a long pair of reins in scarlet wool, and these were used in all his walks abroad. Mrs Berry herself had seen the child tethered by these same red reins to the fence near the back door, so that his mother could keep an eye on him as she worked.

He was a docile child, too languid to protest against his restrictions and, never having known freedom, he accepted his lot with a sweet meekness that the other mothers found pathetic.

Clarence reached the age of six, still cosseted, still adored, still forbidden the company of rough playmates who might harm him. But one bleak December day he fell ill with some childish infection that a normal boy would have thrown off in a day or two. Clarence drooped and died within the week, and the grief of the parents was terrible to see.

Poor Clarence and his red reins! thought Mrs Berry, looking back over the years. She thought of him as 'the sweet dove' that died, in Keats' poem. Long, long ago she had learned it, chanting with the other children at the village school, and still, seventy years on, she could remember it.

> I had a dove, and the sweet dove died;
> And I have thought it died of grieving:
> Oh, what could it grieve for? Its feet were tied
> With a silken thread of my own hand's weaving;
> Sweet little red feet! Why should you die –
> Why should you leave me, sweet bird, why?
> You lived alone in the forest tree,
> Why, pretty thing, would you not live with me?
> I kissed you oft and gave you white peas;
> Why not live sweetly, as in the green trees?

Yes, that was Clarence! 'Tied with a silken thread' of his poor mother's weaving. The stricken parents had moved away soon after the tragedy, and very little was heard of them, although someone once said that the mother had been taken to the madhouse, years later, and was never fit to be released.

Thank God, thought Mrs Berry, turning her pillow, that children were brought up more sensibly these days. She thought of Mary's two vivacious daughters, their glossy hair and round pink cheeks, their exuberance, their inexhaustible energy. Well, they were quiet enough at the moment, though no doubt they would wake early and fill the house with their excitement.

Mrs Berry rearranged the eiderdown, turned her cheek into the pillow, and, thanking God for the blessing of a family, fell asleep at last.

CHAPTER 6

An unaccustomed sound woke the old lady within an hour. She slept lightly these days, and the stirring of one of her granddaughters or the mewing of a cat was enough to make her instantly alert.

She lay listening for the sound again. The wind still moaned and roared outside, the rain pattered fitfully against the windowpane, and the fire whispered as the wood ash fell through the bars of the grate.

It was a metallic noise that had roused her. What could it be? It might possibly be caused by part of the metal trellis which she and Mary had erected against the front porch to aid the growth of a new rose. Could it have blown loose?

But she could have sworn that the sound was nearer at hand, somewhere inside the house. It was not the welcome click of the mousetrap at its work. Something downstairs . . .

She sat upright in the chair. The fire had burned very low, and she leaned forward to put a little more wood on it, taking care to make no noise. Her ears strained for a repetition of the sound.

Now she thought she could hear a slight scuffling noise. A bird? Another mouse? Her heart began to beat quickly. And then the tinny sound again, as though a lid were being lifted from a light saucepan, or a cake tin. Without doubt, someone was in the kitchen!

Mrs Berry sat very still for a minute. She felt no fear, but she was cautious. She certainly did not intend to rouse the sleeping family above. Whoever it was, Mrs Berry felt quite capable of coping with him. Some rough old tramp probably, seeking a dry billet from the storm and, if left alone, on his way before the house stirred at daybreak. Mrs Berry began to feel justifiable annoyance at the thought of some wastrel making free with her accommodation, and, what was more to the point, rifling the larder.

She bent to pick up the poker from the hearth. There was only once chance in ten that she would need to use it, but it was as well to be armed. It gave her extra confidence, and should the man be so silly as to show fight, then she would lay about her with energy and leave him marked.

Tightening her dressing-gown cord round her ample waist, Mrs Berry, poker in hand, moved silently to the door of the living room. This door, then a short passage, and then the kitchen door needed to be negotiated before she came face to face with her adversary. Mrs Berry determined to take the obstacles at a rush, catching the intruder before he had a chance to make his escape.

For one brief moment, before she turned the doorknob, the battered face of an old woman swam into Mrs Berry's mind. The photograph had been given pride of place in the local paper only that week, and showed the victim of some young hooligans who had broken into her pathetic home to take what they could. Well, Mrs Berry told herself sturdily, such things might happen in a town. It wouldn't occur in a little homely place like Shepherds Cross! She had dealt with plenty of scoundrels in her day, and knew that a stout heart was the best defence against bullies. Right would always triumph in the end, and no good ever came of showing fear!

She took a deep breath, a firmer grip on the poker, and flung open the door. Four quick determined steps took her to the kitchen door. She twisted the knob, and pushed the door open with her foot.

There was a stifled sound, something between a sob and a scream, a scuffle, and an unholy clattering as a large tin fell upon the tiles of the kitchen floor.

Mrs Berry switched on the light with her left hand, raised the poker menancingly in her right, and advanced upon her adversary.

Upstairs, Jane stirred. She lay still for a minute or two, relishing the warmth of her sister's back against hers, and the delicious warm hollow in which her cheek rested.

Then she remembered, and sat up. It was just light enough to see that the two empty pillowcases had vanished. She crept carefully out of bed, and went to the foot. There on the floor stood two beautiful knobbly pillowcases, and across each lay an equally beautiful striped stocking.

He had been! Father Christmas had been! Wild excitement was followed by a wave of shame. And she had not seen him! She had fallen asleep, after all her resolutions! It would be a whole year now before she could put Tom Williams' assertion to the test again. She shivered in the cold draught that blew under the door.

Her hands stroked the bulging stocking lovingly. There was the tangerine, there were the sweets, and this must be a dear little doll at the top. If only morning would come! She did not intend to undo the presents now. She would wait until Frances woke.

She crept back to bed, shivering with cold and excitement. She thrust her head into the hollow of her pillow again, leaned back comfortably against her sister, sighed rapturously at the thought of joys to come, and fell asleep again within a minute.

Mrs Berry's stern gaze, which had been directed to a point about six feet from the ground, at a height where her enemy's head should reasonably have been, now fell almost two feet to rest upon a pale, wretched urchin dressed in a streaming wet rain-coat.

At his feet lay Mrs Berry's cake tin, luckily right way up, with her cherished Madeira cake exposed to the night air. The lid of the cake tin lay two yards away, where it had crashed in the turmoil.

'Pick that up!' said Mrs Berry in a terrible voice, pointing imperiously with the poker.

Snivelling, the child did as he was told, and put it on the table.

'Now the lid!' said Mrs Berry with awful emphasis. The boy sidled nervously towards it, his eyes fixed fearfully upon the menacing poker. He retrieved it and replaced it fumblingly, Mrs Berry watching the while.

The floor was wet with footmarks. The sodden towel had been pushed aside by the opening door. Mrs Berry remembered with a guilty pang that she had forgotten to lock the door amidst the general excitement of Christmas Eve.

She looked disapprovingly at the child's feet, which had played such havoc upon the kitchen tiles. They were small, not much bigger than Jane's, and clad in a pair of sneakers that squelched with water every time the boy moved. He had no socks, and his legs were mauve with cold and covered with goose pimples.

Mrs Berry's motherly heart was smitten, but no sign of softening showed in her stern face. This boy was nothing more than a common housebreaker and thief. A minute more and her beautiful Madeira cake, with its artistic swirl of angelica across the top, would have been demolished – gulped down by this filthy ragamuffin.

Nevertheless, one's Christian duty must be done.

'Take off those shoes and your coat,' commanded Mrs Berry, 'and bring them in by the fire. I want to know more about you, my boy.'

He struggled out of them, and picked them up in a bundle in his arms. His head hung down and little droplets of water ran from his bangs down his cheeks.

Mrs Berry unhooked the substantial striped roller towel from the back of the door and motioned to the boy to precede her to the living room.

'And don't you dare to make a sound,' said Mrs Berry in a fierce whisper. 'I'm not having everyone woken up by a rapscallion like you.'

She prodded him in the back with the poker and followed her reluctant victim to the fireside.

He was obviously completely exhausted and was about to sink into one of the armchairs, but Mrs Berry stopped him.

'Oh, no you don't, my lad! Dripping wet, as you are! You towel yourself dry before you mess up my furniture.'

The boy took the towel and rubbed his soaking hair and wet face. Mrs Berry studied him closely. Now that she had time to look at him, she saw that the child was soaked to the skin. He was dressed in a T-shirt and grey flannel shorts, both dark with rain-water.

'Here, strip off,' commanded Mrs Berry.

'Eh?' said the boy, alarmed.

'You heard what I said. Take off those wet clothes. Everything you've got on.'

The child's face began to pucker. He was near to tears.

'Lord, boy,' said Mrs Berry testily, 'I shan't look at you. In any case, I've seen plenty of bare boys in my time. Do as you're told, and I'll get you an old coat to put on while your things dry.'

She stood a chair near the fire and hung the child's sodden coat across the back of it. His small sneakers were placed on the hearth, on their sides, to dry.

The boy slowly divested himself of his wet clothing, modestly turning his back towards the old lady.

She thrust more wood upon the fire, looking at the blaze with satisfaction.

'Don't you dare move till I get back,' warned Mrs Berry, making for the kitchen again. An old duffel coat of Jane's hung there. It should fit this skinny shrimp well enough. Somewhere too, she remembered, a pair of shabby slippers, destined for the next jumble sale, were tucked away.

She found them in the bottom of the shoe cupboard and returned to the boy with her arms full. He was standing shivering by the fire, naked but for the damp towel round his loins.

He was pathetically thin. His shoulder blades stuck out like little wings, and every rib showed. His arms were like sticks, his legs no sturdier, and they were still, Mrs Berry noticed, glistening with water.

'Sit down, child,' she said, more gently, 'and give me that towel. Seems you don't know how to look after yourself.'

He sat down gingerly on the very edge of the armchair, and Mrs Berry knelt before him rubbing energetically at the skinny legs. Apart from superficial mud, Mrs Berry could see that the boy was basically well cared for. His toe nails were trimmed, and his scarred knees were no worse than most little boys'.

She looked up into the child's face. He was pale with fatigue and fright, his features sharp, the nose prominent; his small mouth, weakly open, disclosed two slightly projecting front teeth. Mouselike, thought Mrs Berry, with an inward shudder, and those great ears each side of the narrow pointed face added to the effect.

'There!' said Mrs Berry. 'Now you're dry. Put your feet in these slippers and get this coat on you.'

The child did as he was told in silence, fumbling awkwardly with the wooden toggle fastenings of the coat.

'Here, let me,' said Mrs Berry, with some exasperation. Deft herself, she could not abide awkwardness in others. The boy submitted to her ministrations, holding up his head meekly, and gazing at her from great dark eyes as she swiftly fastened the top toggles.

'Now pull that chair up close to the fire, and stop shivering,' said Mrs Berry briskly. 'We've got a lot to talk about.'

The boy did as he was bidden, and sat with his hands held out to the blaze. By the light of the fire, Mrs Berry observed the dark rings under the child's eyes and the open drooping mouth.

'Close your mouth and breathe through your nose,' Mrs Berry told him. 'Don't want to get adenoids, do you?'

He closed his mouth, swallowed noisily, and gave the most appallingly wet sniff. Mrs Berry made a sound of disgust, and struggled from her chair to the dresser.

'Blow your nose, for pity's sake!' she said, offering him several paper handkerchiefs. He blew noisily, and then sat, seemingly exhausted by the effort, clutching the damp tissue in his skinny claw.

'Throw it on the back of the fire, child,' begged

Mrs Berry. 'Where on earth have you been brought up?'

He looked at her dumbly and, after a minute, tossed the handkerchief towards the fire. He missed and it rolled into the hearth by the steaming sneakers. Mrs Berry suddenly realized that she was bone tired, it would soon be one o'clock, and that she wished the wretched child had chosen some other house to visit at such an hour. Nevertheless, duty beckoned, and she girded herself to the task.

'You know what you are, don't you?' she began. The boy shook his head uncomprehendingly.

'You are a burglar and a thief,' Mrs Berry told him. 'If I handed you over to the police, you'd get what you deserve.'

At this the child's dark eyes widened in horror.

'Yes, you may well look frightened,' said Mrs Berry, pressing home the attack. 'People who break into other people's homes and take their things are nothing more than common criminals and have to be punished.'

'I never took nothin',' whispered the boy. With a shock, Mrs Berry realized that these were the first words that she had heard him utter.

'If I hadn't caught you when I did,' replied Mrs Berry severely, 'you would have eaten that cake of mine double quick! Now wouldn't you? Admit it. Tell the truth.'

'I was hungry,' said the child. He put his two hands on his bare knees and bent his head. A tear splashed down upon the back of one hand, glittering in the firelight.

'And I suppose you are still hungry?' observed Mrs Berry, her eyes upon the tear that was now joined by another.

'It's no good piping your eye,' she said bracingly, 'though I'm glad to see you're sorry. But whether 'tis for what you've done, or simply being sorry for yourself, I just don't know.'

She leaned forward and patted the tear-wet hand.

'Here,' she said, more gently, 'blow your nose again and cheer up. I'll go and get you something to eat, although you know full well you don't deserve it.' She struggled from her chair again.

'It won't be cake, I can tell you that,' she told him flatly. 'That's for tea tomorrow – today, I suppose I should say. Do you realize, young man, that it's Christmas Day?'

The boy, snuffling into his handkerchief, looked bewildered but made no comment.

'Well, what about bread and milk?'

A vision of her two little granddaughters spooning up their supper – days ago, it seemed, although it was only a few hours – rose before her eyes. Simple and nourishing, and warming for this poor, silly, frightened child!

'Thank you,' said the boy. 'I like bread and milk.'

She left him, still sniffing, but with the second paper handkerchief deposited on the back of the fire as instructed.

'Not a sound now,' warned Mrs Berry, as she departed. 'There's two little girls asleep up there. And their ma. All tired out and need their sleep. Same as I do, for that matter.'

She cut a thick slice of bread in the cold kitchen. The wind had not abated, although the rain seemed less violent, Mrs Berry thought, as she waited for the milk to heat. She tidied the cake tin away, wondering whether she would fancy the cake at tea time after all its vicissitudes. Had those grubby paws touched it, she wondered?

She poured the steaming milk over the bread cubes, sprinkled it well with brown sugar and carried the bowl to the child.

He was lying back in the chair with his eyes shut, and for a moment Mrs Berry thought he was asleep. He looked so defenceless, so young, and so meekly mouselike, lying there with his pink-tipped pointed nose in the air, that Mrs Berry's first instinct was to tuck him up in her dressing gown and be thankful that he was at rest.

But the child struggled upright, and held out his skinny hands for the bowl and spoon. For the first time he smiled, and although it was a poor, wan thing as smiles go, it lit up the boy's face and made him seem fleetingly attractive.

Mrs Berry sat down and watched him attack the meal. It was obvious that he was ravenously hungry.

'I never had no tea,' said the child, conscious of
Mrs Berry's eyes upon him.

'Why not?'

The boy shrugged his shoulders.

'Dunno.'

'Been naughty?'

'No.'

'Had too much dinner then?'

The child gave a short laugh.

'Never get too much dinner.'

'Was your mother out then?'

'No.'

The boy fell silent, intent upon spooning the last
delicious morsels from the bottom of the bowl.

'I don't live with my mother,' he said at last.

'With your gran?'

'No. A foster mother.'

Mrs Berry nodded, her eyes never moving from the child's face. What was behind this escapade?

'Where have you come from?' she asked.

The boy put the empty bowl carefully in the corner of the hearth.

'Tupps Hill,' he answered.

Tupps Hill! A good two or three miles away! What a journey the child must have made, and in such a storm!

'Why d'you want to know?' said the boy, in a sudden panic. 'You going to send the police there? They don't know nothin' about me runnin' off. Honest! Don't let on, madam, please, madam!'

The 'madam' amused and touched Mrs Berry. Was this how he had been told to address someone in charge of an institution, or perhaps a lady magistrate at some court proceedings? This child had an unhappy background, that seemed certain. But why was he so scared of the police?

'If you behave yourself and show some sense,' said Mrs Berry, 'the police will not be told anything at all. But I want to know more about you, young man.'

She picked up the bowl.

'Would you like some more?'

'Can I?' said the child eagerly.

'Of course,' said Mrs Berry, resting the bowl on one hip and looking down at the boy.

'What's your name?'

'Stephen.'

'Stephen what?'

'It's not my foster mother's name,' said the boy evasively.

'So I imagine. What is it though?'

'It's Amonetti. Stephen Amonetti.'

Mrs Berry nodded slowly, as things began to fall into place.

'So you're Stephen Amonetti, are you? I think I knew your dad some years ago.'

She walked slowly from the room, sorting out a rag bag of memories, as she made her way thoughtfully towards the kitchen.

CHAPTER 7

Amonetti!

Pepe Amonetti! She could see him now, as he had first appeared in Beech Green during the final months of the last war. He was a very young Italian prisoner of war, barely twenty, and his dark curls and sweeping black eyelashes soon had all the village girls talking.

He was the youngest of a band of Italian prisoners allotted to Jesse Miller, who then farmed a large area at Beech Green. He was quite irrepressible, bubbling over with the joy of living – doubling relishing life, perhaps, because of his short time on active service.

As he drove the tractor, or cleared a ditch, or slashed back a hedge, he sang at the top of his voice, or chattered in his pidgin English to any passer-by.

The girls, of course, did not pass by. The string of compliments, the flashing glances, the expressive hands, slowed their steps. Pepe, with his foreign beauty, stood out from the local village boys like some exotic orchid among a bunch of cottage flowers. In theory, he had little spare time for such dalliance. In practice, he managed very well, with a dozen or more willing partners.

The young lady most in demand at Beech Green at that time was a blonde beauty called Gloria Jarvis.

The Jarvises were a respectable couple with a

string of flighty daughters. Gloria was one of the youngest, and had learned a great deal from her older sisters. The fact that the air base nearby housed several hundred eager young Americans generous with candy, cigarettes and nylon stockings had hastened Gloria's progress in the art of making herself charming.

As was to be expected, 'them Jarvis girls' were considered by the upright members of the community to be 'a fair scandal, and a disgrace to honest parents.' Any man, however ill-favoured or decrepit, was reckoned to be in danger from their wiles, and as soon as Pepe arrived at Beech Green it was a foregone conclusion that he would fall prey to one of the Jarvis harpies.

'Not that he'll put up much of a fight,' observed one middle-aged lady to her neighbour. 'Got a roving eye himself, that lad.'

'Well,' replied her companion indulgently, 'you knows what these foreigners are! Hot blooded. It's all that everlasting sun!'

'My Albert was down with bronchitis and chilblains all through the Italian campaign,' retorted the first lady. 'No, you can't blame the climate for their goings-on. It's just that they're made that way, and them Jarvis girls won't cool their blood, that's for sure.'

It was not long before Pepe's exploits, much magnified in conversations among scandalized matrons, were common knowledge in the neighbourhood, and it was Gloria Jarvis who was named as being the chief object of his attentions.

Gloria may have lost her heart to Pepe's Latin charms, but she did not lose her head. An Italian prisoner of war had little money to spend on a girl, and Gloria continued to see a great deal of her American admirers who spent more freely. Those of them who knew about Pepe dismissed the affair good-naturedly. Gloria was a good-time girl, wasn't she? So what?

Pepe, on the other hand, resented the other men's attentions, and became more and more possessive as time went by. He certainly had more hold over the wayward Gloria than his rivals, and though she tossed her blonde Edwardian coiffure and pretended indifference, Gloria was secretly a little afraid of Pepe's passion.

The war ended in 1945, a few months after their first meeting, and Pepe elected to stay on in England as a farm worker. By this time, a child was on the way, and Gloria and Pepe were married at the registry office in Caxley.

Their first child, a girl, had Pepe's dark good looks. A blonde boy, the image of his mother, appeared a year later, and the family began to be accepted in Beech Green. Pepe continued to work for Jesse Miller and to occupy one of his cottages.

For a few years all went well, and then Pepe vanished. Gloria and the two children had a hard time of it, although Jesse Miller kindheartedly allowed them to continue to live in the cottage. It was during these difficult days that Mrs Berry had got to know Gloria better.

She was vain, stupid and a slattern, but she was also abandoned and in despair. Mrs Berry helped her to find some work at a local big house, and now and again looked after the children to enable Gloria to go shopping or to visit the doctor. The old Jarvises were dead, by now, and the older sisters were little help.

Mrs Berry showed Gloria how to make simple garments for the children, taught her how to knit and, more useful still, how to choose the cheap cuts of meat and cook them so that a shilling would stretch to its farthest limit.

Happily married herself, Mrs Berry urged Gloria to find Pepe and make it up, if only for the sake of the family. But it was two years before the errant husband was traced, and another fifteen months before he could be persuaded to return.

He had found work in Nottingham, and came back to Beech Green just long enough to collect Gloria and the children, their few poor sticks of furniture and their clothes. They left for Nottingham one grey December day, but Pepe had found time to call at Mrs Berry's and to thank her for all she had done.

Handsomer than ever, Pepe had stood on her doorstep, refusing to come in, his eyes shy, his smile completely disarming. No one, least of all Mrs Berry, could have remained hostile to this winning charmer with his foreign good manners.

'I did nothing – no more than any other neighbour,' Mrs Berry told him. 'But now it's your concern, Pepe. You see you treat her right and make a fresh start.'

'Indeed, yes. I do mean to do that,' said Pepe earnestly. He thrust his hand down inside his greatcoat and produced a ruffled black kitten, which he held out to Mrs Berry with a courtly bow.

'Would you please to accept? A thank you from the Amonettis?'

Mrs Berry was taken aback but rallied bravely.

She knew quite well that the kitten was their own, and that they could not be bothered to take it with them to their new home. But who could resist such a gesture? And who would look after the poor little waif if she did not adopt it?

She took the warm furry scrap and held it against her face.

'Thank you, Pepe. I shall treasure it as a reminder of you all. Good luck now, and mind my words.'

For some time after this Mrs Berry heard nothing of the Amonettis. The kitten, named Pepe after its donor, grew up to be a formidable mouser and was much loved by the Berry family. Years later, someone in Caxley told Mrs Berry that Pepe had vanished yet again, and that Gloria had returned to live with a sister in the county seat twenty miles away. Whilst there, she had had one last brief reconciliation with Pepe, but within a week there had been recriminations, violence and police action.

After this, Pepe had vanished for good, and it was generally believed that this time he had returned to Italy.

The outcome of that short reunion must be Stephen, Mrs Berry thought to herself, as she stood in her draughty kitchen preparing the boy's meal. Gloria's present circumstances she knew from hearsay. She continued to live in one room of her sister's house and was what Mrs Berry still thought of as 'a woman of the streets.' No wonder that the boy had been taken into the care of the local authority. His mother, though to be pitied in some ways, Mrs Berry told herself charitably, was no fit person to bring up the boy, and heaven above knows what the conditions of the sister's house might be! Those Jarvis girls had all been first-class sluts, and no mistake!

Mrs Berry picked up the tray and carried it back to the fireside.

The child's smile was stronger this time.

'You are very kind,' he said, with a touch of his father's grace, reaching hungrily for the food.

She sat back in the armchair and watched the boy. Now that he had eaten and was getting warm, the pinched look, which sharpened his mouselike features, had lessened. His cheeks glowed pink and his lustrous dark eyes glanced about the room as he became more relaxed. Given time, thought Mrs Berry, this boy could become as bewitching as his father. But, at the moment, he was unhappy. What could have sent the child out into such a night as this? And furthermore, what was to be done about it?

Mrs Berry bided her time until the second bowlful had vanished, then took up the poker. The boy looked apprehensive, but Mrs Berry, ignoring him, set the poker about its legitimate business of stirring the fire into a blaze, and then replaced it quietly.

'Now,' she said, in a businesslike tone, 'you can just explain what brings you into my house at this time of night, my boy.'

There was a long pause. In the silence, the clock on the mantel shelf struck two and a cinder clinked into the hearth. The wind seemed to have shifted its quarter slightly, for now it had found a crevice by the window and moaned there as if craving for admittance.

'I'm waiting,' said Mrs Berry ominously. The boy's thin fingers fidgeted nervously with the toggle fastenings. His eyes were downcast.

'Not much to tell,' he said at last, in a husky whisper.

'There must be plenty,' replied Mrs Berry, 'to bring you out from a warm bed on Christmas Eve.'

The child shook his head unhappily. Tears welled up again in the dark eyes.

'Now, that's enough of that!' said the old lady. 'We've had enough waterworks for one night. If you won't tell me yourself, you can just answer a few questions. And I want the truth, mind!'

The boy nodded, and wiped his nose on the back of his hand. Mrs Berry pointed in silence to the paper hankies beside him. Meekly, he took one and dried his eyes.

'You say you live at Tupps Hill?'

The child nodded.

'Who with?'

A look of fear crept over the mouselike face.

'You tellin' the police?'

'Not if you tell me the truth.'

'I live at Number Three. With Mrs Rose.'

'Betty Rose? And her husband's Dick Rose, the roadman?'

'That's right.'

Mrs Berry digested this information, whilst the child took advantage of the lull in the interrogation to turn his shoes in the hearth. They were drying nicely.

Mrs Berry tried to remember all she knew about the Roses. They had been married some time before her own girls, she seemed to recall, and Betty's mother had been in good service at Caxley. Other than that, she knew little about them, except that they were known to be a respectable honest pair and regular churchgoers. Dick Rose was a slow methodical fellow, who would never rise above his present job of road sweeper in Caxley, from what Mrs Berry had heard.

'Any children?' she asked.

'Two!' replied the boy. He looked sulky. Was this the clue? Was the child jealous for some reason?

'How old?'

'Jim's eleven, two years older 'n me. Patsy's eight, nearly nine. A bit younger 'n me.'

That would be about right, thought Mrs Berry, trying to piece the past together from her haphazard memories, and the child's reluctant disclosures.

'You're lucky to live with the Roses,' observed the old lady, 'and to have the two children for company.'

The boy gave a sniff, but whether in disgust or from natural causes it was impossible to say.

'You get on all right?'

'Sometimes. Patsy tags on too much. Girls is soppy.'

'They've usually got more sense than boys,' retorted Mrs Berry, standing up for own sex. 'You notice it isn't Patsy who's run out into a storm and got into trouble.'

The child stuck out his lower lip mutinously but said nothing. The drenched raincoat was now steaming steadily, and Mrs Berry turned it on the back of the chair. The boy's thin T-shirt, which had been hanging over the fire screen, was now dry, and Mrs Berry smoothed it neatly into shape on her knee before folding it.

'Patsy's got a watch,' said the boy suddenly.

'Has she now?'

'So's Jim. They both got watches. Patsy and Jim.'

'For Christmas, do you mean?'

'No, no!' said the child impatiently. 'Patsy had hers in the summer, for her birthday. Jim had his on his birthday. Last month it was.'

'They were lucky.'

She waited for further comment, but silence fell again. The boy was clearly upset about something, some injustice connected with the watches, some grievance that still rankled. His fingers plucked nervously at a piece of loose cotton on the hem of the duffel coat. His face was thunderous. Pepe's Latin blood was apparent as his son sat there brooding by the fire.

'They're their own kids, see?' said the boy, at length. 'So they give 'em watches. I reckon my real mum'd give me one – just like that, if I asked her.'

Light began to break through the dark puzzle in Mrs Berry's mind.

'Do you know where she is?'

The child looked up, wide eyed with amazement.

'Course I do! She's with me auntie. I sees her once a month. She says she'll have me back, soon as she's got a place of her own. Ain't no room at auntie's, see?'

Mrs Berry did see.

'I want to know more about these watches. When is your birthday?'

'Second of February.'

'Well, you might be lucky too, and get a watch then.'

'That's what *they* say!' said the boy with infinite scorn in his voice. His head was up now, his eyes flashing. The mouse had become a lion.

'If they means it,' he went on fiercely, 'why don't they let me have it for Christmas? That's what I asked 'em.'

'And what did they say?'

'Said as there was too much to buy anyway at Christmas. Couldn't expect a big present like a watch. I'd 'ave to wait and see.'

'Fair enough,' commented Mrs Berry. The Roses had obviously done their best to explain matters to the disappointed child.

'No, it ain't fair enough!' the child burst out. 'Dad Rose, 'e gets extra money Christmastime – a bonus they calls it. *And* all his usual pay. They could easy afford one little watch. The other two've got theirs. Why should I have to wait? I'll tell you why!'

He leaned forward menacingly. Mrs Betty could see why Pepe had had such a hold over poor stupid Gloria Jarvis. Those dark eyes could be very intimidating when they flashed fire.

'Because I'm only the foster kid, that's why! They gets paid for havin' me with 'em, but they won't give me a watch, same as their own kids 've got. They don't care about me, that's the truth of it!'

The tears began to flow again, and Mrs Berry handed him a paper hanky in silence. It was coming out now – the whole, sad, silly, simple little story. Soon she would know it all.

'I thought about it when I got to bed,' sniffed Stephen Amonetti, mopping his eyes. 'Soon as Jim was asleep, I crept out. They never heard me go. They was watching the telly. Never heard nothing. I knows the way.'

'Where to?'

'Me mum, of course. She'd understand. I bet she'd give me a watch for Christmas, *and* let me stay with her too, if she knowed how I was feeling.

Anyway, you wants your own folk at Christmastime.
I fair hates the Roses just now.'

He blew his nose violently, threw the hanky to the
back of the fire as instructed, and flopped back in
the chair, with a colossal shuddering sigh. The duffel
coat fell apart, displaying his skinny bare legs. His
hands drooped from the arms of the chair.

Mrs Berry stooped to put another log on the fire,
before beginning her lecture. That done, she settled
back in the armchair.

'As far as I can see,' she began severely, 'you are a
thoroughly silly, spoiled little boy.'

She glanced across at her visitor and saw that she
was wasting her breath.

Utterly exhausted, his pink mouse nose pointing
towards the ceiling and pink mouse mouth ajar, Mrs
Berry's captive was deep in slumber.

CHAPTER 8

Upstairs in her draughty bedroom Mary stirred. Some faint noise had penetrated the thick folds of sleep that wrapped her closely. Too tired to open her eyes or to sit up, she tried bemusedly to collect her thoughts.

Could she have heard voices? She remembered that her mother was below. Perhaps she had turned on the little radio set for company, she told herself vaguely.

Should she go and inspect the mousetrap? The bed was seductively warm, her limbs heavy with sleep. To stir outside was impossible. Besides, she might wake the children as well as her mother.

Exhausted, she turned over, relishing the comfort of her surroundings after the bustle of the day. She began to slip back into unconsciousness, and her last remembrance of Christmas Eve was the sight of Ray Bullen's smile as he hoisted young Frances on to the bus.

With a feeling of warm contentment, Mary drifted back to sleep.

Old Mrs Berry rearranged the eiderdown and put her tired head against the back of the chair. Through half-closed eyes she surveyed her visitor.

He was snoring slightly, and Mrs Berry's maternal instinct made her want to approach the boy and quietly close his mouth. It was shameful the way some people let their children grow up to be mouth breathers – leading the way to all sorts of infections in later life, besides encouraging snoring, an unnecessary complication to a shared bedroom. Why, Mrs Berry could recall, from when she was in service, many a shocking case among the gentry of couples agreeing to separate bedrooms simply on account of snoring!

However, on this present occasion, Mrs Berry proposed to let sleeping dogs lie. The child was not her permanent responsibility. But Betty Rose ought to look into the matter herself, and quickly, before the habit grew worse.

Her thoughts hovered round the events that had led to the boy's presence under her roof. As far as she could judge, the boy was sensibly cared for by the Roses, who seemed to have tackled the child's grievance sympathetically.

There was no doubt in Mrs Berry's mind that the child was far better off where he was than with that fly-by-night mother of his. As for thinking that she would have him back permanently to live with her – well, that was just wishful thinking on the child's part. The local authority would not allow that, especially in the sordid circumstances in which Gloria now appeared to live and work.

Stephen Amonetti! Mrs Berry mused, her eyes still on her visitor. He would not be an easy child to bring up, with Pepe and Gloria as parents. She pitied the Roses, and commended them for having the pluck to take on this pathetic outcome of a mixed marriage. He would need a firm hand, and plenty of affection too, to right the wrongs the world had done him. It could not be easy for the Roses, trying to be fair to their own two and to fit this changeling into their family.

She remembered Pepe's quick jealousy of Gloria's earlier rivals. Plainly, this child was as quick to resentment as his father had been. She remembered the fury in those dark eyes as the boy spoke of the watches. That smouldering jealousy was a legacy from his Latin father. The thought-lessness, culminating in the flight from home, care-less of the feelings of others, was a legacy from his casual mother.

This boy was going to be a handful, unless someone pulled him to his senses, thought Mrs Berry. The Roses, respectable people though they were, might well be too gentle with the child, too ineffectual, although they apparently were doing their best to cope with this cuckoo in their nest. After all, Dick Rose left home early in the morning and was late back at night. It would fall upon Betty's shoulders, this responsibility, and with two children of her own to look after the task might be too great for her.

The child had been thinking on the wrong lines for too long, Mrs Berry told herself. He had har-boured grievances, resented authority, and indulged in self-pity. The old lady, with the strong principles instilled by her Victorian upbringing, condemned such wrong-headedness roundly. That the child was the victim, to a certain extent, of his circumstances, she was ready to concede, but the matter did not end there. She was heartily sick of the modern theories that condoned wrongdoing on the grounds that the wrongdoers were to be pitied and not blamed.

Every individual, she firmly believed, had the freedom of choice between good and evil. If one were so wicked, or thoughtless, or plain stupid enough to choose to do evil, then one must be prepared to take the consequences. Children, naturally, had to be trained and helped to resist temptation and to choose the right path, but to consider them as always in the right, as so many people nowadays seemed to do, was to do them a disservice, thought old Mrs Berry.

Her own children had been brought up with clear standards. Little Amelia Scott had learned the virtues early, from the plaque in the church extolling modesty and economy, from her upright parents, and from the strict but kindly teachings of the village schoolteachers, the Scriptures and the vicar of the parish. These stood her in good stead when she became a mother.

She had also been told of the things which were evil: lying, boasting, stealing, cruelty and loose living and thinking. It seemed to Mrs Berry that in these days evil was ignored. Did modern parents and teachers think that by burying their heads in the sand, evil would vanish? It had to be faced today, as bravely as it always had been in the past. It was there, plain for all to see, in the deplorable accounts of murder, bloodshed, violence and exploitation appearing in newspapers and shown on every television screen. The trouble was, thought Mrs Berry, that too often it was shrugged off as 'an aspect of modern living', when it should have been fought with the sword of righteousness, as she and her generation had been taught to do.

It was a great pity that the seven deadly sins were not explained to the young these days. There, asleep in the chair, was the victim of one of them – Envy. Had he been brought up to recognize his enemies in time, young Stephen might have been safely asleep in his own bed, instead of lying there caught in a web of his own weaving.

For, one had to face it, Mrs Berry told herself, this self-indulgence in envy and self-pity had led the boy to positive wrongdoing. He was, in the eyes of the law and all right-thinking people, a burglar and a would-be thief.

He was also guilty of disloyalty to the Roses, who were doing their best to bring him up. And he had completely disregarded the unhappiness this flight might cause them.

All this she intended to make clear to the child as soon as he awoke. But there was a further problem – a practical one. How could she get the child home again without involving her own family or the Roses?

Would they have missed him yet? Would they have rung the police? As soon as the child woke, she would try and find out the usual practice at night in the Roses' house. Would they on Christmas eve have put the children's presents on their beds, as she and Mary had done? If so, would they have noticed that the boy was missing from their son's side?

All this must be discovered. Meanwhile, it was enough that the boy was resting. She too would close her eyes for a catnap. They both needed strength to face what was before them.

She dropped, thankfully, into a light doze.

★

The boy woke first. Bending to feel his drying shoes, he knocked the poker into the hearth. This small clatter roused the old lady.

She was alert at once, as she always was when she woke up, despite her age.

The clock stood at twenty minutes past three, and although the wind still moaned at the window, there seemed to be no sound of rain pattering on the pane. The worst of the storm appeared to be over.

Mrs Berry felt the raincoat. It was practically dry. She carefully turned the sleeves inside out and re-arranged the garment so that it had the full benefit of the fire's heat.

It was very cosy in the room. Refreshed by her nap, the old lady looked with approval at the two red candles on the mantelpiece waiting to be lit at teatime – today, Christmas Day, the day they had prepared for, for so long.

The Christmas tree sparkled on the side table. The paper chains, made by the little girls' nimble fingers, swayed overhead and the holly berries glimmered as brightly as the fire itself.

'Merry Christmas!' said Mrs Berry to the boy.

'Thank you. Merry Christmas,' he responded. 'It don't seem like Christmas, somehow.'

'I'm not surprised. You haven't made a very good start with it, have you?'

Stephen shook his head dismally.

'What's more,' continued the old lady, 'you've put your poor foster parents, and me, to a mint of worry and trouble, by being such a wicked, thoughtless boy.'

'I'm sorry,' said the child. There was something

perfunctory about the apology which roused Mrs Berry's ire.

'You *say* it,' she said explosively, 'but do you *mean* it? Do you realize that all this trouble stems from your selfishness? You've been given a good home, food, warmth, clothes, comfort, taken into a decent family, and how do you repay the Roses? You ask for something you know full well is too expensive for them to give you, and then you sulk because it's not forthcoming!'

The boy opened his mouth as though to protest against this harangue, but Mrs Berry swept on.

'You're a thoroughly nasty, mean-spirited little boy, eaten up with envy and jealousy, and if you don't fight against those things you're going to turn into a real criminal. You understand what I say?'

'Yes, but I never –'

'No excuses,' continued Mrs Berry briskly. 'You see what your sulking and envy led you to – breaking into my house and helping yourself to my Madeira cake. Those are crimes in themselves. If you were a few years older, you could be sent to prison for doing that.'

The child suddenly bent forward and put his head in his hands. She could see that he was fighting tears, and remained silent, watching him closely, and hoping that some of her words of wisdom had hit their mark.

'Have you ever had a spanking?' she asked suddenly.

'Only from me real mum. She gave me a clout now and again. The Roses don't hit none of us.'

'They're good people, better than you deserve, I

suspect. I warrant if you'd been my little boy, you'd have had a few smacks by now, to show you the difference between right and wrong.'

There was a sniffing from the hidden face, but no comment. Mrs Berry's tone softened.

'What you've got to do, my child, is to start afresh. You've seen tonight where wickedness and self-pity lead you. For all we know, Mr and Mrs Rose are distracted – their Christmas spoiled – just because you must have your own way. And if they've told the police, then that's more people upset by your thoughtlessness.

'No, it's time you thought about other people instead of yourself. Time you counted your blessings, instead of making yourself miserable about things you covet. No selfish person is ever happy. Remember that.'

The boy nodded, and lifted his head from his hands. His cheeks were wet, and his expression was genuinely penitent.

'What we've got to do now,' said Mrs Berry, 'is to put things right as quickly and quietly as we can. Tell me, do you think the Roses will have missed you?'

The child looked bewildered.

'They don't never look in once they've tucked us up. They calls out, softlike, "Good night," when they goes to bed but don't open the door.'

'Not even on Christmas Eve?' asked Mrs Berry, broaching the subject delicately. Did the child still believe in Father Christmas? He had had enough to put up with this night, without any further painful disclosures.

'We has our presents on the breakfast table,' said

Stephen, catching her meaning at once. 'And our stockings at teatime, when we light the candles on the Christmas tree.'

'So they may not know you left home?'

'I don't see how they can know till morning.'

'I see.'

Mrs Berry fell silent, turning over this fact in her mind. There seemed to be every hope that the child was right. If so, the sooner he returned, and crept back to bed, the better. It seemed proper in her straightforward mind, that having done wrong the boy himself should put it right. She discounted the wrong done against herself and her own property, although she sincerely hoped that the child had learned his lesson. It was his attitude to his foster parents, and to all others with whom he must work and live, that must be altered.

'Do you go to church?' asked Mrs Berry.

'To Sunday school. Sometimes we go to Evensong.'

'Then you've heard about loving your neighbour.'

The child looked perplexed.

'Is it a commandment? We had to learn ten of those once, off of the church wall, at Sunday school.'

'It's another commandment: "Love thy neighbour as thyself." Do you understand what it means?'

The child shook his head dumbly.

'Well, it sums up what I've been telling you. Think about other people and their feelings. Consider them as much as you consider yourself. Put yourself in your foster parents' place, for instance.

How would you feel if the boy you looked after was so discontented that he ran away, making you feel that you had let him down, when all the time you had been doing your level best to make him happy?'

The boy looked at his hands, and said nothing.

'You're going to go back, Stephen, and get into that house as quietly as you can, and get into bed. Can you do it?'

'Of course. The larder window's never shut. I've been in and out dozens of times.'

'And you say nothing at all about what has happened tonight. It's a secret between you and me. Understand?'

'Yes,' he whispered.

'There's no need for anyone to be upset by this, except you. I hope you'll have learned your lesson well enough to be cheerful and grateful for all that you are given, and all that's done for you, on Christmas Day. Do you promise that?'

The boy nodded. Then his eyes grew round, as he looked at Mrs Berry in alarm.

'But s'pose they've found out?'

'I was coming to that,' said the old lady calmly. 'You tell them the truth, make a clean breast of it, and say you'll never do it again – and mean it, what's more!'

The child's eyes grew terrified.

'Tell them about coming in here?'

'Of course. And tell them I should like to see them, to explain matters.'

'And the police?'

'If the police have been troubled, then you apologize to them too. You know what I told you. You must face the consequences whatever they are. This night should make you think in future, my boy, and a very good thing too.'

She stood up, and moved to the window. Outside, the rain had stopped, but a stiff wind blew the ragged clouds swiftly across a watery moon, and ruffled the surface of the puddles.

It was a good step to Tupps Hill, but Stephen must be on his way shortly. Mrs Berry was not blind to the dangers of the night for a young child walking the lanes alone, but it was a risk that had to be taken. At least the weather was kinder, the child's clothing was dry, and he had eaten and slept. He had got himself into this situation, and it would do him no harm, thought Mrs Berry sturdily, to get himself out of it. In any case, the chance of meeting anyone abroad at half-past three on Christmas morning was remote.

'Put your clothes on,' directed the old lady, 'while I make us both a cup of coffee.'

She left him struggling with the toggle fastenings as she went into the kitchen. When she returned with the steaming cups of coffee, the boy was lacing his shoes. He looked up, smiling. He was so like Pepe, in that fleeting moment, that the years vanished for old Mrs Berry.

'Lovely and warm,' Stephen said approvingly, holding up his feet.

Mrs Berry handed him his cup, and offered the biscuit tin. As he nibbled his Ginger Nut with his prominent front teeth, Stephen's resemblance to a mouse was more marked than ever.

The old lady shuddered. Was her own little horror, the mouse, still at large above? Mrs Berry craved for her bed. She was suddenly stiff and bone-tired, and longed for oblivion. What a night it had been! Would the boy ever remember anything that she had tried to teach him? She had her doubts, but one could only try. Who knows? Something might stick in that scatterbrained head.

She motioned to the child to fetch his coat, turned the sleeves the right way out, and helped to button it to the neck. His chin was smooth and warm against her wrinkled hand, and reminded her with sudden poignancy of her own sleeping grandchildren.

She held him by the lapels of his raincoat, and looked searchingly into his dark eyes.

'You remember the promise? Say nothing, if they know nothing. Speak the truth if they do. And in future, do what's right and not what's wrong.'

The child nodded solemnly.

She kissed him on the cheek, gently and without smiling. They went to the front door together, Mrs Berry lifting a bar of chocolate from the Christmas tree as she passed.

'Put it in your pocket. You've a long way to go and may get hungry. Straight home, mind, and into bed. Promise?'

'Promise.'

She opened the door quietly. It was fairly light, the moon partially visible through fast-scudding clouds. The wind lifted her hair and rustled dead leaves in the road.

'Good-bye then, Stephen. Don't forget what I've told you,' she whispered.

'Good-bye,' he whispered back.

He stood motionless for a second, as if wondering how to make his farewell, then turned suddenly and began the long trudge home.

Mrs Berry watched him go, waiting for him to turn, perhaps, and wave. But the child did not look back, and she watched him walking steadily – left, right, left, right – until the bend in the lane hid him from her sight.

CHAPTER 9

Back in the warm living room Mrs Berry found herself swaying on her feet with exhaustion. She steadied herself by holding on to the back of the armchair that had been her refuge for the night.

It was years since she had felt such utter tiredness. It reminded her of the days when, as a young girl, she had helped with the mounds of washing at the vicarage. She had spent an hour or more at a time turning the heavy mangle – a monster of cast iron and solid wood – in the steamy atmosphere of the washhouse.

She looked now at her downy nest of feather pillow and eiderdown, and knew that if she sat down sleep would engulf her. She would be stiff when she awoke for every nerve and sinew in her old body craved for the comfort of her bed, with room to stretch her heavy limbs.

She would brave that dratted mouse! Ten chances to one is had made its way home again, and, in any case, she was so tired she would see and hear nothing once she was abed.

She glanced round the room. The fire must be raked through, and the two telltale coffee cups washed and put away. Mrs Berry had no intention of telling Mary and the little girls about her visitor.

She put all to rights, moving slowly, her limbs leaden, her eyes half-closed with fatigue. She drew back the curtains, ready for the daylight, and scanned the stormy sky.

The moon was high now. Ragged clouds skimmed across its face, so that the glimpses of the wet trees and shining road were intermittent. The boy should be well on his way by now. She hoped that he had avoided the great puddles that silvered his path. Those shoes would be useless in this weather.

The old lady sighed, and turned back to the armchair, folding the eiderdown neatly and putting the plump pillow across it. Gathering up her bundle, she took one last look at the scene of her encounter with young Stephen. Then, shouldering her burden, she opened the door to the staircase and went, very slowly, to her bedroom.

Exhaustion dulled the terror that stirred her at the thought of the mouse still at large. Nevertheless, the old lady's heart beat faster as she quietly opened the bedroom door. The great double bed was as welcome a sight as a snug harbour to a storm-battered boat.

Mary had turned down the bedclothes. They gleamed, smooth and white as a snowdrift, in the faint light of the moon.

The room was still and cool after the living room. Mrs Berry stood motionless, listening for any scuffle or scratching that might betray her enemy. But all was silent.

She switched on the bedside lamp, which had been Mary's last year's Christmas present. It had a deep-pink shade that sent a rosy glow into the room. The old lady replaced her pillow and spread out the eiderdown, then, nerving herself, she bent down stiffly to look under the bed and see if the intruder was still there.

All was as it should be. She scanned the rest of the floor, and saw the mousetrap. It was empty, and the second piece of cheese was still untouched.

Mrs Berry's spirits rose a little. Surely, this might mean that the mouse had returned to his own home? He would either have been caught, or the cheese would have been eaten, as before. But the trap must not be left there, a danger to the grandchildren, who would come running in barefoot, all too soon, to show their tired grandmother the things that Father Christmas had brought.

Mrs Berry took a shoe from the floor and tapped the trap smartly. The crack of the spring snapping made her jump but now all was safe. She could not bring herself to touch the horrid thing with her bare fingers, but prodded it to safety, under the dressing table, with her shoe.

Sighing with relief, the old lady climbed into bed, drew up the bedclothes and stretched luxuriously.

How soon, she wondered, before Stephen Amonetti would be enjoying his bed, as she did now?

At the rate he was stepping out, thought Mrs Berry drowsily, he must be descending the long slope that led to the fold in the downs at the foot of Tupps Hill.

She knew that road well. The meadows on that southern slope had been full of cowslips when little Amelia Scott and her friends were children. She could smell them now, warm and sweet in the May sunshine. She loved the way the pale green stalks grew from the flat rosettes of leaves, so like living pen wipers, soft and fleshy, half hidden in the springy grass of the downland.

The children made cowslip balls as well as bunches to carry home. Some of the mothers made cowslip wine, and secretly young Amelia grieved to see the beautiful flowers torn from their stalks and tossed hugger-mugger into a basket. They were too precious for such rough treatment, the child felt, though she relished a sip of the wine when it was made, and now tasted it again on her tongue, the very essence of a sunny May day.

On those same slopes, in wintertime, she had tobogganed with those same friends. She remembered a childhood sweetheart, a black-haired charmer called Ned, who always led the way on his homemade sled and feared nothing. He scorned gloves, hats, and all the other winter comforts in which loving mothers wrapped their offspring, but rushed bareheaded down the slope, his eyes sparkling, cheeks red, and the breath blowing behind him in streamers.

Poor Ned, so full of life and courage! He had gone to a water-filled grave in Flanders' mud before he was twenty years old. But the memory of that vivacious child remained with old Mrs Berry as freshly as if it were yesterday that they had swept down the snowy slope together.

In those days a tumbledown shack had stood by a small rivulet at the bottom of the slope. It was inhabited by a poor, silly, old man, called locally Dirty Dick. He did not seem to have any steady occupation, although he sometimes did a little field work in the summer months, singling turnips, picking the wild oats from the farmers' standing corn, or making himself useful when the time came round for picking apples or plums in the local orchards.

The children were warned not to speak to him. Years before, it seemed, he had been taken to court in Caxley for some indecent conduct, and this was never forgotten. The rougher children shouted names after him and threw stones. The more gently nurtured, such as little Amelia, simply hurried by.

'You're not to take any notice of him,' her mother had said warningly.

'Why not?'

A look of the utmost primness swept over her mother's countenance.

'He is sometimes a very *rude* old man,' she said, in a shocked voice.

Amelia inquired no further.

His end had been tragic, she remembered. He had been found, face downwards, in the little brook, a saucepan in his clenched hand as he had dipped water to boil for his morning tea. The doctor had said his heart must have failed suddenly. The old man had toppled into the stream and drowned in less than eight inches of spring flood water.

Young Amelia had heard of his death with mingled horror and relief. Now she need never fear to pass that hut, dreading the meeting with 'a very *rude* old man', whose death, nevertheless, seemed unnecessarily cruel to the soft-hearted child.

Well, Stephen Amonetti would have no Dirty Dick to fear on his homeward way, but he would have the avenue to traverse, a frightening tunnel of dark trees lining the road for a matter of a hundred yards across the valley. Even on the hottest day, the air blew chill in those deep shadows. On a night like this, Mrs Berry knew well, the wind would clatter the branches and whistle eerily. Stephen would need to keep a stout heart to hold the bogies at bay as he ran the gauntlet to those age-old trees.

But by then he would be within half a mile of his home, up the steep short hill that overlooked the valley. A small estate of council houses had been built at Tupps Hill, some thirty years ago, and though the architecture was grimly functional and the concrete paths gave an institutional look to the area, yet most of the tenants – countrymen all – had softened the bleakness with climbing wall plants and plenty of bright annuals in the borders.

The hillside position, too, was enviable. The houses commanded wide views over agricultural land, the gardens were large and, with unusual forethought, the council had provided a row of garages for their tenants, so that unsightly, old shabby cars were screened from view. Those lucky enough to get a Tupps Hill house were envied by their brethren.

If only Stephen could get in unobserved! Mrs Berry stirred restlessly, considering her visitor's chances of escaping detection. Poor little mouse! Poor little Christmas mouse! Dear God, please let him creep into his home safely!

And then she froze. Somewhere, in the darkness close at hand, something rustled.

Her first instinct was to snatch the eiderdown from the bed, and bolt. She would fly downstairs again to the safety of the armchair, and there await the dawn and Mary's coming to her rescue.

But several things kept her quaking in the warm bed. Extreme tiredness was one. Her fear that she would rouse the sleeping household was another. The day ahead would be a busy one, and Mary needed all the rest she could get. This was something she must face alone.

Mrs Berry tried to pinpoint the position of the rustling. A faint squeaking noise made her flesh prickle. What could it be? It did not sound like the squeak of a mouse. The noise came from the right, by the window. Could the wretched creature be on the windowsill? Could it be scrabbling, with its tiny claws, on the glass of the windowpane, in its efforts to escape?

Mrs Berry shuddered at the very thought of confronting it, of seeing its dreadful stringy tail, its beady eyes, and its more than likely darting to cover into some inaccessible spot in the bedroom.

All her old terrors came flying back, like a flock of

evil black birds, to harass her. There was that ghastly dead mouse in her aunt's flour keg, the next one with all those pink hairless babies in her father's toolbox, the one that the boys killed in the school lobby, the pair that set up home once under the kitchen sink, and all those numberless little horrors that Pepe the cat used to bring in, alive and dead, to scare her out of her wits.

But somehow, there had always been someone to cope with them. Dear Stanley, or Bertie, or brave Mary, or some good neighbour would come to her aid. Now, in the darkness, she must manage alone.

She took a deep breath and cautiously edged her tired old legs out of bed. She must switch on the bedside lamp again, and risk the fact that it might stampede the mouse into flight.

Her fingers shook as she groped for the switch. Once more, rosy light bathed the room. Sitting on the side of the bed, Mrs Berry turned round to face the direction of the rustling, fear drying her throat.

There was no sound now. Even the wind seemed to have dropped. Silence engulfed the room. Could she have been mistaken? Could the squeaking noise have been caused by the thorns of the rosebush growing against the wall? Hope rose. Immediately it fell again.

For there, crouched in a corner of the windowsill, was a tiny furry ball.

Old Mrs Berry put a shaking hand over her mouth to quell any scream that might escape her unawares. Motionless, she gazed at the mouse. Motionless, the mouse gazed back. Thus transfixed, they remained.

Only the old lady's heavy breathing broke the silence that engulfed them.

After some minutes, the mouse lifted its head and snuffed the air. Mrs Berry caught her breath. It was so like Stephen Amonetti, as he had sprawled in the armchair, head back, with his pointed pink nose in the air. She watched the mouse, fascinated. It seemed oblivious of danger and sat up on its haunches to wash its face.

Its bright eyes, as dark and lustrous as Stephen's, moved restlessly as it went about its toilet. Its minute pink paws reminded Mrs Berry of the tiny pink shells she had treasured as a child after a Sunday-school outing to the sea. It was incredible to think that something so small could lead such a full busy life, foraging, making a home, keeping itself and its family fed and cleaned.

And that was the life it must return to, thought Mrs Berry firmly. It must go back, as surely as Stephen had, to resume its proper existence. Strange that two creatures, so alike in looks, should flee their homes and take refuge on the same night, uninvited, under her roof!

The best way to send this little scrap on its homeward journey would be to open the window and hope that it would negotiate the frail stairway of the rosebush trained against the wall, and so return to earth. But the thought of reaching over the mouse to struggle with the window catch needed all the courage that the old lady could muster, and she sat on the bed summoning her strength.

The longer she watched, the less frightened she became. It was almost like watching Stephen Amonetti all over again – a fugitive, defenceless, young, and infinitely pathetic. They both needed help and guidance to get them home.

She took a deep breath and stood up. The bed springs squeaked, but the mouse did not take flight. It stopped washing its whiskers and gazed warily about it. Mrs Berry, gritting her teeth, approached slowly.

The mouse shrank down into a little furry ball, reminding Mrs Berry of a fur button on a jacket of her mother's. Quietly, she leaned over the sill and lifted the window catch. The mouse remained motionless.

The cold air blew in, stirring the curtain and bringing a breath of rain-washed leaves and damp earth.

Mrs Berry retreated to the bed again to watch developments. She sat there for a full minute before her captive made a move.

It raised its quivering pink nose and then, in one bound, darted over the window frame, dragging its pink tail behind it. As it vanished, Mrs Berry hurried to the window to watch its departure.

It was light enough to see its tiny shape undulating down the crisscross of thorny rose stems. But when it finally reached the bare earth, it was invisible to the old lady's eyes.

She closed the window carefully, sighed with relief and exhaustion, and clambered, once more, into bed.

Her two unbidden visitors – her Christmas mice – had gone! Now, at long last, she could rest.

Behind the row of wallflower plants, close to the bricks of the cottage, scurried the mouse, nose twitching. It ran across the garden path, dived under the cotoneaster bush, scrambled up the mossy step by the disused well, turned sharp right through the jungle of dried grass beside the garden shed, and streaked, unerringly, to the third hawthorn bush in the hedge.

There, at the foot, screened by ground ivy, was its hole. It dived down into the loose sandy earth, snuffling the dear frowsty smell of mouse family and mouse food.

Home at last!

At much the same time, Stephen Amonetti lowered himself carefully through the pantry window.

The house was as silent as the grave, and dark inside, after the pallid glimmer of the moon's rays.

With infinite caution he undid the pantry door, and closed it behind him. For greater quietness, he removed his wet shoes and, carrying them in one hand, he ascended the staircase.

The smells of home were all about him. There was a faint whiff of the mince pies Mrs Rose had made on Christmas Eve mingled, from the open door of the bathroom, with the sharp clean smell of Lifebuoy soap.

Noiselessly, he turned the handle of the bedroom door. Now there was a stronger scent – of the liniment that Jim used after football, boasting, as he rubbed, of his swelling muscles. The older boy lay curled on his side of the bed, dead to the world. It would take more than Stephen's entry into the room to wake him.

Peeling off his clothes, Stephen longed for bed,

for sleep, for forgetfulness. Within three minutes, he was lying beside the sleeping boy, his head a jumble of cake tins, fierce old ladies, stormy weather, sore feet.

And somewhere, beyond the muddle, a hazy remembrance of a promise to keep.

CHAPTER 10

It was light when Mrs Berry awoke. She lay inert in the warm bed, relishing its comfort, as her bemused mind struggled with memories of the night.

The mouse and Stephen! What a double visitation, to be sure! No wonder she was tired this morning and had slept late. It must be almost eight o'clock – Christmas morning too! Where were the children? Where was Mary? The house was uncommonly quiet. She must get up and investigate.

At that moment, she heard footsteps outside in the road, and the sound of people greeting each other. Simultaneously, the church bell began to ring. Yes, it must be nearly eight o'clock, and those good parishioners were off to early service!

Well, thought Mrs Berry philosophically, she would not be among the congregation. She rarely missed the eight o'clock service, but after such a night she would be thankful to go later, at eleven, taking the two little girls with her.

She struggled up in bed and gazed at the sky. It was a glory of grey and gold: streamers of ragged clouds, gilded at their edges, filled the world with a luminous radiance, against which the bare twigs of the plum tree spread their black lace.

She opened the window, remembering with a shudder the last time she had done so. Now the air, fresh and cool, lifted her hair. The bells sounded clearly, as the neighbours' footsteps died away into the distance.

'Awake then?' said Mary, opening the door. 'Happy Christmas!'

She bore a cup of tea, the steam blowing towards her in the draught from the window.

'You spoil me,' said Mrs Berry. 'I ought to be up. Proper old sleepyhead I am today. Where are the children?'

'Downstairs, having breakfast. Not that they want much. They've been stuffing sweets and the tangerines from their stockings since six!'

She put the cup on the bedside table and closed the window.

'They wanted to burst in here, but I persuaded them to let you sleep on. What happened to the mouse? Is it still about? I see the trap's sprung.'

'I let it out of the window,' said Mrs Berry. She could not keep a touch of pride from her voice.

'You never! You brave old dear! Where was it then?'

'On the sill. I got so tired by about three, I risked it and came up. I don't mind admitting I fair hated reaching over the little creature to get at the latch, but it made off in no time, so that was all right.'

'That took some pluck,' said Mary, her voice warm with admiration. 'Can I let those rascals come up now, to show you their presents?'

'Yes, please,' said Mrs Berry, reaching for her cup. 'Then I'll get up, and give you a hand.'

Mary called down the staircase, and there was a thumping of feet and squeals and shouts as the two excited children struggled upstairs with their loot.

'Look, Grandma,' shouted Frances, 'I've put on my slippers!'

'Look, Grandma,' shouted Jane, 'Father Christmas brought me a dear little doll!'

They flung themselves upon the bed, Mary watching them with amusement.

'Mind Gran's tea,' she warned.

'Leave them be,' said her mother lovingly. 'This is how Christmas morning should begin!'

Smiling, Mary left the three of them and went downstairs.

On the door mat lay an envelope. Mary's heart sank, as she bent to pick it up. Not another person they'd forgotten to send to? Not another case of Mrs Burton all over again? Anyway, it was too late now to run about returning Christmas cards. Whoever had sent it must just be thanked when they met.

She took it into the living room and stood with her back to the fire, studying the face of the envelope with some bewilderment. Most of the cards were addressed to 'Mrs Berry and Family,' or to 'Mrs Berry and Mrs Fuller,' but this was to 'Mrs Bertie Fuller' alone, and written in a firm hand.

Wonderingly, Mary drew out the card. It was a fine reproduction of 'The Nativity' by G. van Honthorst, and inside, beneath the printed Christmas greetings, was the signature of Ray Bullen. A small piece of writing paper fluttered to the floor, as Mary, flushing with pleasure, studied the card.

She stooped to retrieve it. The message it contained was simple and to the point.

> I have two tickets for the New Year's Eve concert at the Corn Exchange. Can you come with me? Do hope so!
>
> RAY

Mary sat down with a thud on the chair recently vacated by young Jane. Automatically, she began stacking the girls' bowls sticky with cornflakes and milk. Her hands were shaking, she noticed, and she felt shame mingling with her happiness.

'Like some stupid girl,' she scolded herself, 'instead of a widow with two girls.'

She left the crockery alone, and took up the note again. It was kind of him – typical of his thoughtfulness. Somehow, he had managed to write the card after seeing her yesterday, and had found someone in the village who would drop it through her letterbox on the way to early service. It must have taken some organizing, thought Mary, much touched. He was a good sort of man. Bertie had always said so, and this proved it.

As for the invitation, that was a wonderful thing to have. She would love to go and knew that her mother would willingly look after the children. But would she approve? Would she think she was being disloyal to Bertie's memory to accept an invitation from another man?

Fiddlesticks! thought Mary robustly, dismissing such mawkish sentiments. Here was an old friend offering to take her to a concert – that was all. It was a kindness that would be churlish to rebuff. Of course she would go, and it would be a rare treat too!

Calmer, she rose and began to take the dishes into the kitchen, her mind fluttering about the age-old problem of what to wear on such a momentous occasion. There was her black, but it was too funereal, too widowlike. Suddenly she wanted to look gay, young, happy – to show that she appreciated the invitation, she told herself hastily.

There was the yellow frock she had bought impulsively one summer day, excusing her extravagance by persuading herself that it was just the thing for the Women's Institute outing to the theatre. But when the evening had arrived she had begun to have doubts. Was it, perhaps, too gay for a widow? Would the tongues wag? Would they say she was 'after' someone? Mutton dressed as lamb?

She had put it back in the cupboard, and dressed herself in the black one. Better be on the safe side, she had told herself dejectedly, and had felt miserable the whole evening.

Yes, the yellow frock should have an airing, and her bronze evening shoes an extra shine. Ray Bullen should have no cause to regret his invitation.

She turned on the tap, as the children came rushing into the room.

'Why, Mummy,' exclaimed Frances, wide eyed with amazement, *'you're singing!'*

Upstairs Mrs Berry put on her grey woollen jumper and straightened the Welsh tweed skirt. This was her working outfit. Later in the morning she would change into more elegant attire, suitable for churchgoing, but there was housework to be done in the next hour or two. Last of all, she tied a blue and white spotted apron round her waist, and was ready to face the day.

Once more, she opened the window. The small birds chirped and chatted below, awaiting their morning crumbs. A grey and white wagtail teetered back and forth across a puddle, looking for all the world like a miniature curate, with his white collar and dove grey garments. The yellow winter jasmine starred the wall below, forerunner of the aconites and snowdrops soon to come. There was a hopeful feeling of spring in the air, decided Mrs Berry, gazing at the sky. How different from yesterday's gloom!

The children's happiness was infectious. Their delight in the simple presents warmed the old lady's heart and set her thinking of that other child, less fortunate, who had no real family of his own and who had wept because of it.

How was he faring? Had he, after all, found a watch among his parcels? Mrs Berry doubted it. The Roses had spoken truly when they told the child that a watch was too much to expect at Christmas. No doubt, lesser presents would make him happy, assuaging to some extent that fierce longing to have a watch like Patsy's and Jim's. A passionate child, thought Mrs Berry, shaking her head sadly. Pepe all over again! It made life hard for the boy, and harder still for those who had to look after him. Would he ever remember any of the good advice she had tried to offer? Knowing the ways of children, she suspected that most of her admonitions had gone in one ear and out of the other.

Ah well! One could only hope, she thought, descending the staircase.

Mary had set a tray at the end of the table for her mother. Beyond it stood the pink cyclamen and a pile of parcels. The two children, hopping from leg to leg with excitement, hovered on each side of the chair.

'Come on, Gran! Come and see what you've got. Mum gave you the plant!'

'Mary,' exclaimed Mrs Berry, hands in the air with astonishment, 'you shouldn't have spent so much money on me! What a beauty! And so many buds to come out too. Well, I don't know when I've seen a finer cyclamen, and that's a fact.'

She kissed her daughter warmly. Why, the girl seemed aglow! Christmas was a comforting time, for old and young, thought Mrs Berry, reaching out for the parcels.

'Open mine first,' demanded Frances.

'No, mine,' said Jane. 'I'm the oldest.'

'I'll open them together,' said the old lady, taking one in each hand. 'See, I'll tear this bit off this one, then this bit off that one –'

She tugged at the wrappings gently.

'No, no!' cried Jane, unable to bear the delay. 'Do one first – don't matter which – then the other. But read the tags. We wrote 'em ourselves.'

Mrs Berry held the two tags at arm's length. Her spectacles were mislaid amidst the Christmas debris.

'"Darling Grandma, with love from Jane,"' she read aloud. She shook the parcel, then smelled it, then held it to her ear. The children hugged each other in rapture.

'Why do you listen to it?' queried Frances. 'Do you think there's a bird in it?'

'A watch perhaps,' said Mrs Berry, surprised by her own words.

'A *watch*?' screamed the girls. 'But you've got a watch!'

'So I have,' said Mrs Berry calmly. 'Well, let's see what's in here.'

Wrapped in four thicknesses of tissue paper was a little eggtimer.

'Now, *that*,' cried the old lady, 'is *exactly* what I wanted. Clever Jane!'

She kissed the child's soft cheek.

'Now mine!' begged Frances. 'Quick! Undo it *quick*, Gran.'

'I must read the tag. "Dear Gran, Happy Christmas, Frances." Very nice.'

'Undo it!' said the child.

Obediently, the old lady undid the paper. Inside was a box of peppermint creams.

'My favourite sweets!' said Mrs Berry. 'What a kind child you are! Would you like one now?'

'Yes please,' both said in unison.

'I hoped you'd give us one,' said Frances, beaming. 'Isn't it lucky we like them too?'

'Very lucky,' agreed their grandmother, proffering the box.

'Let Gran have her breakfast, do,' Mary said, appearing from the kitchen.

'But she's got lots more parcels to open!'

'I shall have a cup of tea first,' said the old lady, 'and then undo them.'

Sighing at such maddening adult behaviour, the two children retired to the other end of the table where they had set out a tiny metal tea set of willow pattern in blue and white.

'This is my favourite present,' announced Frances, 'and the teapot pours. See?'

Mary and her mother exchanged amused glances. The set had been one of several small toys they had bought together in Caxley to fill up the stockings. The chief present for each girl had been a doll, beautifully dressed in handmade clothes worked on secretly when the girls were in bed. It was typical of children the world over that some trifle of no real value should give them more immediate pleasure than the larger gifts.

At last, all the presents were unwrapped. Bath cubes, stockings, handkerchiefs, sweets, a tin of biscuits, another of tea, and a tablecloth embroidered by Mary – all were displayed and admired. Mary's presents had to be brought from the sideboard and shown to her mother, to please the two children, despite the fact that Mrs Berry had seen most of them before.

'Now, what's to do in the kitchen?' asked Mrs Berry, rising from the table.

'Nothing. The pudding's in, and the bird is ready, and the vegetables.'

'Then I'll dust and tidy up,' declared Mrs Berry. 'Upstairs first. I can guess what the girls' room looks like!'

'At least there are no mice!' laughed Mary.

The children looked up, alert.

'No mice? Was there a mouse? Where is it now?'

Their grandmother told them about the intruder, and how she had settled by the fire, but at last gone up to bed and had let the mouse out of the window.

What would they have said, she wondered, as she told her tale, if she had told them the whole story? How their eyes would have widened at the thought of a boy – a *big* boy of nine – breaking into their home and trying to steal their grandmother's Madeira cake! As it was, the story of the real mouse stirred their imagination.

'I expect it was hungry,' said Jane with pity. 'I expect it smelled all the nice Christmas food and came in to have a little bit.'

'It had plenty of its own sort of food outdoors,' Mrs Berry retorted tartly.

'Perhaps it just wanted to see inside a house,' suggested Frances reasonably. 'You shouldn't have frightened it away, Gran.'

'It frightened *me* away,' said the old lady.

'Perhaps it will come back,' said Jane hopefully.

'That,' said her grandmother forcefully, 'I sincerely hope it will not do.'

And she went upstairs to her duties.

When the children and her mother had departed to church, the house was blessedly quiet. Mary, basting the turkey and turning potatoes in the baking dish, had time to ponder her invitation. As soon as the children were safely out of the way she would have a word with their mother, then reply.

But where should she send it? There had been no address on the note, and although she knew the part of Caxley in which Ray lived, she could not recall the name of the road, and certainly had no idea of the number. Perhaps the best thing would be to send it to the office of *The Caxley Chronicle*, where he worked. He would be going into work, no doubt, on the day after Boxing Day. Plenty of time to spare before New Year's Eve.

Now that the first initial surprise of the invitation was over, Mary found herself growing more and more delighted at the thought of the evening outing. Caxley had produced a New Year's Eve concert as long as she could remember, and she and Bertie had attended several of them.

The Corn Exchange was always full. It was something of an occasion. The mayor came, all the local gentry sat in the front rows, and everyone knew that the music provided would be good rousing stuff by Handel and Bach and Mozart, with maybe a light sprinkling of Gilbert and Sullivan, or Edward German, or Lionel Monckton, as a garnish.

It was definitely a social affair, when one wore one's best, and hoped to see one's friends and be seen by them. It would be good, thought Mary, to have a personable man as an escort instead of attending a function on her own.

Kind Ray! Good Quaker Ray! How did that passage go in the library book – 'Very thoughtful and wealthy and good'? She could vouch for two of those virtues anyway!

She slammed the oven door shut and laughed aloud.

At one o'clock the Christmas dinner – everything done to a turn – was set upon the table, and the two little girls attacked their plates with enviable appetite. Their elders ate more circumspectly.

Nevertheless, at two o'clock it was the children who played energetically on the floor with their new toys, whilst Mary and her mother lay back in their armchairs and succumbed to that torpor induced by unaccustomed rich food.

'We must take a turn in the fresh air before it gets dark.' Mrs Berry yawned; Mary nodded agreement drowsily.

They woke at three, much refreshed, donned their coats and gloves, and set off. The bright clouds of morning had gone; a gentle grey light veiled the distant scene.

The four of them walked towards the slope where young Stephen had walked scarcely twelve hours earlier. Mrs Berry's mind was full of memories of her Christmas visitor. She strode along, dwelling on the oddity of events that had brought one of the Amonetti family into her life once more.

Ahead of her, holding a child by each hand, Mary was running a few steps, then stopping suddenly to bring the two children face to face in an ecstatic embrace. It was a game they had loved as toddlers, but it was years, thought Mrs Berry, since Mary had played it with them.

Their delighted screams matched the calling of the flight of rooks above, slowly winging homewards against the evening sky.

Now they had reached the top of the slope, and Mary, breathless, stopped to wait for her mother.

They stood together looking across the shallow valley, already filling with the pale mist of winter.

'That's Tupps Hill over there, isn't it?' said Mary. Her mother nodded.

'D'you remember the Roses?'

'Vaguely,' said Mary. 'Why?'

There was an intensity about her mother's gaze that made Mary curious.

The old lady did not answer for a moment, her eyes remained fixed upon the shadowy hill beyond the rising mist.

'I might call on them one day,' she said, at last.

'Not yet awhile. But some day – some day, perhaps.'
She turned suddenly. 'Let's get home, Mary dear.
There's no place like it – and it's getting cold.'

CHAPTER 11

It was hardly surprising, at teatime, to find that the family's appetite was small, despite the afternoon walk.

'I'll just bring in the Christmas cake,' said Mary, 'and the tea tray. Though I expect you'd like a slice of your Madeira, wouldn't you?'

'No, thank you,' replied Mrs Berry hastily.

She pondered on the fate of the Madeira cake as Mary clattered china in the kitchen. It certainly seemed a terrible waste of sugar and butter and eggs, not to mention the beautiful curl of angelica that cost dear knows how much these days. But there it was. The thought of those pink paws touching it was enough to put anyone off the food.

Perhaps she could cut off the outside, and slice the rest for a trifle? Waste was something that Mrs Berry abhorred. But at once she dismissed the idea. It was no good. The cake must go. No doubt the birds would relish it, but she must find an opportunity for disposing of it when Mary was absent from the scene. Explanations would be difficult, under the circumstances.

Mary returned with the tray. To the accompaniment of cries of appreciation from the children the candles were lighted on the Christmas tree and at each end of the mantelpiece.

Outside, the early dusk had fallen, and the shadowy room, lit by a score of flickering candle flames and the glow from the fire, had never looked so snug and magical, thought Mrs Berry. If only their menfolk could have been with them . . .

She shook away melancholy as she had done so often. The time for grieving was over. There was much to be thankful for. She looked at Mary, intent upon cutting the snowy cake, and the rosy children, their eyes reflecting the light from the candles, and she was content.

And that child at Tupps Hill? Was he as happy as her own? She had a feeling that he might be – that perhaps he had been able to let the Christmas spirit soothe his anxious heart.

Jane's Christmas cracker had yielded a tiny spinning top that had numbers printed on it. When it came to rest, after being twirled on the table, the number that was uppermost gave the spinner his score. This simple toy provided part of the evening's play time, and all four played.

Later, Mrs Berry played Ludo with the children – a new game found in Frances' pillow slip – while Mary wrote some thank-you letters. By seven o'clock both children were yawning, although they did their best to hide this weakness from the grown-ups. It would be terrible to miss anything on this finest day of the year.

'Bed,' said Mary firmly, and as the wails greeted her dictum, she relented enough to say: 'You can take your toys upstairs and play with them for a little while.'

Within half an hour, they were safely in bed, and Mary and her mother sat down to enjoy the respite from the children's clamour.

'Why, there's a new Christmas card!' exclaimed Mrs Berry, her eye lighting on Mary's from Ray.

Mary rose to fetch it from the mantelpiece and handed it to her mother.

'Someone dropped it through the letterbox first thing this morning. I bumped into Ray yesterday when we were shopping and he helped us on to the bus with our parcels.'

'Typical of the Bullens,' commented Mrs Berry, studying the card with approval. 'I knew his mother when she was young. A nice girl.'

Mary took a breath. This seemed as propitious a time as any other to mention the invitation.

'There is a note somewhere. He has asked me to go to the New Year's Eve concert. Would you mind? Looking after the girls, I mean?'

'Good heavens, no! I'm glad to think of you getting out a little. You'll enjoy an evening with Ray Bullen,' said her mother easily.

Mrs Berry leaned back in the chair and closed her eyes. It had been a long day, and she was near to sleep. A jumble of impressions, bright fragments of the last twenty-four hours, jostled together in her tired mind like the tiny pieces of coloured glass in a child's kaleidoscope.

Stephen's mousey face, his pink hand spread like a starfish upon his knee, with a shining tear upon it. Her own shadow, poker in hand, monstrously large on the passage wall as she approached the unknown intruder. The furry scrap crouched on the window-sill with the wild weather beyond. Stephen's resolute back, vanishing round the bend of the lane as he marched home. The reflection of the candles in her grandchildren's eyes. The candles in the church – dozens of them today – and the sweet clear voices of the choir boys.

She woke with a jerk. The clock showed that she had slept for ten minutes. Her last impression still filled her mind.

'It was lovely in church this morning,' she said to Mary. 'Flowers and candles, and the boys singing so sweetly. You should have come.'

'I will next Sunday,' Mary promised. 'A New Year's resolution, Mum.'

There was a quiet happiness about Mary that did not escape Mrs Berry's eyes, but in her wisdom she said nothing.

Things, she knew in her bones, were falling, delicately and rightly, into place.

★

'I'll go and tuck up the girls,' said Mrs Berry, struggling from her chair, 'and switch off their light.'

She mounted the stairs and was surprised to see that both children were in her own room. They were kneeling on her bed, very busy with something on the windowsill.

They turned at her approach.

'We're just putting out a little supper for the Christmas mouse,' explained Jane.

On the ledge was one of the doll's tin willow pattern plates. Upon it were a few crumbs of Christmas cake and one or two holly berries.

'They're apples for him,' said Frances. 'When people call you should always offer them refreshment, Mummy says.'

Mrs Berry remembered the steaming bowl of bread and milk clutched against a duffel coat.

'She's quite right,' she said, smiling at them. 'But somehow I don't think that mouse will come back.'

Stephen's dwindling figure, striding away, came before her eyes. The children looked at her, suddenly forlorn. She offered swift comfort.

'But I'm sure of one thing. That Christmas mouse will remember his visit here for the rest of his life.'

The rising moon silvered the roofs at Shepherds Cross and turned the puddles into mirrors. The sky was cloudless. Soon the frost would come, furring the grass and hedges, glazing the cattle troughs and water butts.

Dick Rose, at Tupps Hill, was glad to get back to the fireside after shutting up the hens for the night.

The table had been pushed back against the wall,

and the three children were crawling about the floor, engrossed in a clockwork train that rattled merrily around a maze of lines set all over the floor. Betty sat watching them, as delighted as they were with its bustling manoeuvres.

'It's only fell off once,' said Stephen proudly, looking up at his foster father's entrance.

'Good,' said Dick. He never wasted words.

'Are you sad Father Christmas never brought you a watch?' asked Patsy of Stephen. Dick's eyes met his wife's.

Patsy was still young enough to believe in the myth, and the boys had nobly resisted enlightening her.

Stephen turned dark eyes upon her.

'Never thought about it,' he lied bravely. 'I've got all this, haven't I?'

He picked up the little train, and held it, whirring, close to his face. He turned and smiled – the radiant warm smile of his lost father – upon his foster parents.

'You're a good kid,' said Dick gruffly. 'And your birthday ain't far off.'

For the first time since Stephen's tempestuous arrival, he thought suddenly, the boy seemed part of the family.

There was a stirring beneath the third bush in the hawthorn hedge. A sharp nose pushed aside the ground-ivy leaves, and the mouse emerged into the moonlight.

It paused, sniffing the chill air, then ran through the dry grass by the shed, negotiated the mossy step by the wellhead, and stopped to nibble a dried seed pod.

On it ran again, parting the crisp grass with its sinuous body, diving down ruts, scrambling up slopes, until it gained the wet earth behind the wall-flower plants.

Between the plants and the brick wall of the cottage it scampered, until it reached the foot of the rosebush, where it stopped abruptly. Far, far above it, lights glowed from the windows.

A tremor shook its tiny frame. Its nose and whiskers quivered at the sense of danger, and it turned to double back on its tracks, away from the half-remembered terrors of an alien world.

It hurried out into the moonlight and made for the open field beyond the hawthorn hedge. There among the rimy grass and the sweet familiar scents, its panic subsided.

Nibbling busily, safely within darting distance of its hole, the Christmas mouse was at peace with its little world.